I0626152

Just Gone

BRIAN COLBORNE

JUST GONE

BRIAN COLBORNE

- 1 -

Alexandria, Virginia

Rob excused himself from the meeting as his phone vibrated in his pocket. Nobody ever called him and he wondered what would cause someone to ring him up over and over again like that.

"Rob Marshall," he said as he answered.

"Rob, it's me. You have to get to the school now!"

"Honey, slow down. What's wrong?"

"It's Alex! Oh my God. Oh my God!"

"Gina, for God's sake, what is it?"

"Alex is gone, Rob. They can't find him and..." Gina's voice seemed to trail off. Rob realized that he had dropped his phone and he picked it up.

"I'm on my way." He didn't wait for an answer and hung up as he sped toward the elevator. After he repeatedly pressed the button in vain, he headed for the stairs. His body barely kept up with his feet as they thundered down the stairs, flight after flight. By the time Rob reached his car, the sound of his racing heart pulsated in his head. He fumbled with his keys and he had barely turned over the engine before the car was in gear, headed toward parking garage exit.

Rob drove as fast as he could. He didn't care if he broke any laws. He had to get to the school as fast as he could. He weaved his way through the traffic as best as he could and ignored the angry car horns as he sped past them. Each bend in the road pushed and pulled his body from side to side. Rob wasn't sure if he passed by any police cars along the way, but he wouldn't have stopped if he did. He would have let them throw on their sirens and clear a path for him, consequences be damned.

Rob arrived at the school and yanked the keys out of the ignition before he ran through the front doors. He sprinted toward the office and almost collided with his wife and the principal as he turned a corner.

"Rob! Thank God you're here," Gina wrapped her arms around her husband. Rob held his wife close, but his eyes were fixed upon Mrs. Weaver, the principal, as she primped her suit jacket, ever the steadfast professional. Rob wanted to scream at her, but instead he put his hands on Gina's shoulders and released her from his embrace.

"Any news?" Rob said. Gina shook her head and pressed a tissue to her eyes. Her mascara had been wiped and smeared so much that it made her look like she'd been awake for weeks.

"We've looked all over the school. Alex isn't here. We can't find him anywhere." Gina leaned against Rob again. Mrs. Weaver cleared her throat and gestured toward her office. Two police officers took notes as they spoke to Alex's teacher. The receptionist rifled through files and drawers.

"Come inside, Mr. and Mrs. Marshall," Mrs. Weaver said. Rob held a chair for his wife, but didn't take a seat for himself. Mrs. Weaver sat down and straightened her suit jacket as she exhaled.

"What the hell happened?" Rob said before Mrs. Weaver could begin.

"Rob, please," Gina said. "Go on, Mrs. Weaver."

"Mr. and Mrs. Marshall, we are doing everything we can to find Alex. The police are already looking for him. They have his description, but it would be better if they had a recent photograph. Do either of you have one with you?" Rob took a picture out of his wallet and pushed it across the desk. Mrs. Weaver stood up and called the two officers over. They came in and introduced themselves. One of them left with the picture. The taller one shut the door and looked at Rob.

"Folks, I want you to know that we have units searching the area on foot and on the roads in all possible directions. We'll get that picture out to all of them right away." Rob turned to Mrs. Weaver.

"What happened?" he said. Mrs. Weaver leaned on her forearms.

"After recess, his teacher did a head count and realized Alex wasn't there. She had seen him a few minutes before and assumed he went inside. She notified me immediately and, as part of our protocol, I notified the police," she said.

"You know he has a tendency to wander off, we told you that! Who was watching him? You're sure he's not in the school?" Rob said. Mrs. Weaver nodded.

"I'm sure."

The police officer stepped closer to the desk.

"If I may, I'm going to suggest you folks

head back home."

"You're joking, right?" Rob said.

"No, sir. Often times a child will head straight home. We already have an officer waiting, but you should be there if Alex does come back." Gina nodded along with a hopeful glint in her eyes as the officer spoke. Rob felt entirely powerless. He wanted to tear the school apart and rip open every possible door or closet that Alex could have gotten into. He wanted to do *something*.

"I'll meet you there," the officer said. "I'm going to want to ask you some more questions if it's OK." Against his instinct, Rob agreed. He took Gina to her car and she assured him that she was fine to get home on her own.

He sat down in his car and stared at the playground. The bell rang to end the day and children filed out of the doors. Rob's eyes darted around as the children met their parents who had come to pick them up; blissfully ignorant of the day's events. Every red jacket caught Rob's focus, but none of them was his son's. He slammed his fist against the dashboard and headed home. The six and a half minute drive felt like hours and when he turned onto the quiet little street they lived on, he panicked. His neighbors busied themselves in their yards to catch a glimpse of the commotion on the sleepy little side road. The street was lined with police cruisers and black SUVs. The police didn't drive those black trucks. The FBI was at his house.

Rob parked a few houses down and walked past all the cruisers and trucks, aware but numb to the eyes that watched him from the porches and lawns. He walked through the front door and found his wife on the couch in tears, surrounded by police and federal agents, a red jacket clutched in her arms.

Alex's red jacket.

- 2 -

All the bodies in Rob's house stopped in place for a moment when he entered. The police talked with the agents and two women sat next to Gina. Rob noticed that Alex's red jacket was actually in a plastic evidence bag and his stomach felt like it flipped upside down inside of him. Rob wanted to ask so many questions, but he couldn't get any words out. Gina stood up from the couch with the bag in her grasp.

"Rob. They found this on the road a few blocks from the school", she said before broke down in tears again. Rob's instinct moved him to his wife and he took the jacket from her hands. His heart raced and his hands numbed when he held it. He looked at the agents who were with his wife on the couch.

"What does this mean?" he said. The blonde one stood up first.

"Mr. Marshall, I'm Agent Dana Brown." She pointed at the dark haired woman. "This is Agent Lane. Can we talk somewhere in private?" Brown reached for the bag and Rob's limp hands released it to her and she handed it off to a man in a navy blue windbreaker. Gina led them all to the dining room table. On the way, Rob saw one of the feds connect the telephone up to a machine that was covered in lights and switches. When they all sat down, Rob questioned the agents right away.

"Please, tell me what's going on," he said. "Why is the FBI here?" Lane clasped her hands together and looked Rob in the eyes. She had the calm voice and caring eyes of a mother.

"The police found the jacket on the road while they were out searching. They also got a 911 from a woman who claimed to have seen the whole thing." One of the cops poked his head in as he walked by.

"The thing is," the officer said, "that lady calls 911 all the time over nothing. We got some guys over there now, though. Just—"

"Yes, thank you, officer," Brown interrupted and held her hand up to dismiss him. Gina looked at Agent Lane with wide eyes.

"What whole thing?" she said.

"We are in the process of getting any information from her that may help but, based on all of the evidence, we have to treat this as a kidnapping," Lane said. "That's why the police called us in. We're with a special unit in the bureau called the Child Abduction Rapid Deployment," she said pointed to the big yellow initials printed on her jacket. "We issued an AMBER Alert once we had reason to believe that Alex had been taken."

"Media's here!" someone called out from the front room

"The media?" Gina stood up and looked around. Agent Brown stood as well.

"It's alright, Mrs. Marshall," she said. "We need their help."

Rob sat there and rubbed his hands together. He couldn't believe what he heard. It all seemed so insane. These things didn't happen around here; they didn't happen to them. If he could only wake up from this horrible dream, he would run into Alex's room and hold him in his arms, but Agent Brown's voice drew him back toward the nightmare of reality.

"Mr. and Mrs. Marshall, we're going to

need you to do something for us. It's not going to be easy, but it can really help."

"What can we do?" Rob said.

"Do you have a hairbrush of Alex's?"

"A hairbrush?"

"We want to eliminate his DNA sample and check his jacket," Brown said, her tone cold and factual.

"It's in the bathroom," Gina said. "Follow me." She led Agent Brown away and Rob stood up. He paced back and forth as he tried to cling to his sanity. Agent Lane might have spoken to him, but if she did, he didn't hear her. He felt himself repeatedly fill with rage and deflate to a withered shell of himself in every agonizing silent moment. He had to do something. Anything. Gina came back with Agent Brown and they all sat back down.

"If you think you can, we'd like you talk to the media," Lane said.

"What?" Rob said.

"You wouldn't have to answer any questions. Just talk about Alex. Show his picture. Make sure that whoever has him sees what he means to you."

"Do you think it will work?" Gina said.

"We have to try," Agent Brown said.

"Don't worry. I'll help you get ready," Lane said. "Do you have a big picture of Alex?" Rob nodded and took her to the hallway. He took the school portrait down from the wall. He ran his fingers across Alex's smiling face and slumped back against the wall. He slid down and sat there, right in the hallway, with Alex's picture clutched in his hands. As Brown stood over him, Rob broke down at that moment. He couldn't hold himself together anymore. Rage gave way to helplessness. He overheard one of the police officers tell the agent about the witness they had interviewed.

"Mr. Marshall?" Lane said.

"Rob," he said, his eyes still fixed on the photograph. "Just call me Rob."

"I want to ask you some questions, Rob."

"Fine," he said. Lane crouched down to his level.

"Is there anyone you can think of that might have a reason to try and hurt you?"

"No."

"Any enemies or someone who might be angry with you?"

"No."

"Is there anyone that Alex might have trusted enough to get in a car with them? A relative maybe?"

"Nobody. We moved here from Pittsburgh for my job. No relatives nearby."

"What about friends or coworkers?" Rob shook his head. He was too preoccupied to be of much use. His brain felt like mush. All could think of was what Alex might be thinking. Was he scared? Was he hurt? Was he—?

"...black SUV?" Lane said.

"Sorry, what?"

"Do you know anyone with a black SUV?"

"I don't know. Maybe. This close to DC that's all you ever see driving around." Rob rested his head against the wall with an exhausted sigh. Agent Brown tapped her partner in the shoulder.

"Media's been briefed. They're ready when we are." Brown nodded and stood up.

"Come on, Rob." She held her hand out to him to help him up.

They spent a few minutes to go over what to say to the cameras. Lane suggested that Gina should do the talking. The idea was that the message could be more powerful if it came from the mother. She had to say his name as much as possible and Rob would hold the picture. They had to humanize their son to the kidnapper. *Humanize him?* Rob thought. The notion that Alex could be an object to someone made him feel sick yet it seemed plausible, even likely, to agents like Brown and Lane.

"They're ready for us," Lane said. "Remember, you shouldn't answer any questions from the reporters. If they ask anything, let one of us handle it. Agent Brown will talk to them first. You can do this." Gina nodded her head as Agent Lane spoke.

They were led out through the front door and even though it was still broad daylight, Rob felt blinded by the onslaught of camera flashes as they stepped out. There was an eerie silence for such a large crowd of reporters and camera operators. The clicks and whirrs of the cameras were the only sounds that Rob could hear over the thunder of his own heartbeat as it pounded through his body. His sharp breath blasted from his nose as he tried to keep his composure. It was the only thing he could do to keep himself together. He stood with his arm around his wife while he watched Agent Brown address the crowd. Rob realized that he hadn't heard a word of what she said when she turned around to introduce them. Rob led Gina to the horrid spectacle on their front lawn. He held Alex's picture up in front of his chest with one hand and kept his other arm around Gina. With a gentle squeeze on her shoulder, she lifted her head and spoke.

"This is our wonderful little boy, Alex. He is five years old and we love him very much. Whoever has Alex please find it in your heart to bring him back safe to his family. Alex belongs here. Alex belongs with his family, playing with his classmates, and having fun with his friends. Alex, if you're watching this, mommy and daddy love you and we miss you. We can't wait to see you, snuggle bug. I want you to be brave, Alex. Be a big brave superhero and you'll be home soon. We love you, Alex."

Rob felt a hand on his shoulder and Lane ushered them back toward the house. He heard an uproar from the reporters who wanted to ask them questions, but kept his stride. Agent Brown stayed outside and handled the media. When they got inside, Lane took them to their bedroom to give them a few minutes alone together.

"You guys did great. The media can spread the word very quickly now. I'll be right outside the door if you need me," she said and closed the door behind her. Rob sat with his arm around Gina and rubbed her back in his absent-minded state.

"They're going to do everything they can," Rob said, unsure of what else to say. "We're going to get him back." Gina buried her head in his chest and cried. All Rob could do was rub her back and try to convince himself that what he just said was true. He felt restless and the walls of the room seemed to shrink in around him. The only thing that kept him from leaping up to go and look for Alex was the slow, soft rhythm of his hand as it ran up and down the fabric of Gina's shirt. They stayed like that, on the edge of their bed, for what felt like an hour before someone tapped on the door.

"Yes?" Gina said as she lifted her head and wiped her eyes.

"May I come in?" It was Agent Lane. Rob tapped Gina on the shoulder and pulled away from her.

"I need your help," he said to Lane. She looked surprised by the flung open door.

"Yes, of course," she said. "What do you need?"

"I need to get out of here. I have to go and look for him."

"Mr. Marshall, I really don't—"

"I can't just sit here!" Rob interrupted. Lane flinched at the volume and took a step back. Rob realized his outburst was unwarranted and rubbed his forehead.

"I'm sorry. Please, I have to look for him." Lane held her hands up and conceded.

"It's alright," she said as she looked down the hallway. "I know you want to help, but we need you here in case they call. And your wife really needs you here right now." Rob resigned himself and sat back down on the bed.

"You're right. You're right. What can we do for you, Agent Lane?" Rob said.

"We got word back from the eyewitness and I wanted to keep you in the loop," Lane said. Gina perked up at the possibility of news.

"What did she see? Was it Alex? Is he OK?" she said. Rob tried to grasp her hand but Gina jerked it away like she always did when she didn't want to be calmed down.

"We showed her some pictures and she pointed out Alex," Lane said.

"Well she probably saw his picture on the news," Rob said. "That cop said she was kinda batty, right?" Lane shook her head.

"Alexandria PD was interviewing her while you addressed the media. There's no way she could have known about it." Lane paused for a moment and Gina's body went as limp as a rag doll, hunched over in defeated exhaustion. Agent Brown popped her head in the doorway.

"Lane, the BAU is here."

"OK. Gina, why don't you come with me?" Gina nodded and shuffled away as she dabbed her wet eyes. Rob looked at the stone-faced Agent Brown as she leaned against the tall dresser.

"Let me guess," Rob said. "This is the part where you interrogate us, right? Well, we didn't have anything to do with this." Agent Brown shook her head and sighed through her nose.

"You've seen too many TV shows, Mr. Marshall," she said. "I'm here to help find Alex. That's all that matters to me right now." For some reason, Rob seethed at her concern for his son.

"Like you care," he said as tears rolled down his cheeks. "He's not your little boy. He's just a case for you. It's not like your son was taken."

"Think what you want about me, Rob," she kept her cool but straightened her stance as she fidgeted with a string bracelet on her wrist. "But my boy was taken. A long time ago. And the CARD team didn't exist back then to help find him. Alex is more than just a case. To all of us. And I don't want you to have to go through what I did."

Rob stood up and paced around his bed with his hand on his forehead.

"I'm sorry, I had no idea."

"It's alright," Brown said. "Now, can I ask you some questions?"

"Whatever you think will help."

Rob answered her myriad questions, no matter how trivial they seemed, but by the end he had grown restless. He felt an unstoppable urge to get out of the house and drive. He knew it was a long shot, but he couldn't stay penned up in his home while his little boy was out there.

Once Agent Brown finished her questions, Rob went to the living room. Gina was on the couch with her thumbnail clenched between her teeth as she bobbed her knee up and down in an anxious tempo. There were even more agents and officers in the house than before, all with different acronyms emblazoned on their jackets. FBI, CARD, PD, BAU. They consulted with each other in small groups; their chatter just a distant noise to Rob's ears. He sat down next to his wife and placed his hand on Gina's thigh to stall her fervent shaking. She relaxed her leg and placed her hand on top of Rob's as Agent Lane stood up to look out the window.

"I'm going to update the media," she said. "I'll be right back." Rob nodded and turned to Gina.

"I think I'm gonna go out back and get some fresh air," he said. Gina nodded and resumed her nervous fidgeting.

Rob peered out through a slit in the curtains as Agent Lane strode across the lawn toward the camera-toting vultures camped out in his yard. Once he was sure that they were focused on Lane, he made his exit. His stride was casual but quick. There were enough black trucks and big news vans to conceal him from their view, but he glanced over and caught the eye of one of the reporters. A tap on the shoulder of her shutterbug companion was all it took for the whole gaggle of them to start a frenzied chase as Rob heightened his pace toward his car. He got in, started the engine, and spun the car around with the deft skill of a stunt driver before he drove off down the street. In his rear view, the reporters scrambled toward their vans, but ultimately abandoned their pursuit.

Rob drove straight for the school and searched around the area. He knew Agent Lane was behind the wheel of the black SUV on his tail, but kept his focus on his search. He drove at a slow pace as he checked and double checked the areas that Alex liked to stop at when they took a walk. Every now and then, a red jacket caught his eye and he stopped the car in an abrupt lurch forward.

Rob pulled into the parking lot of a small playground not far from the school and slowed to a stop. Some children played on the slide and others jumped around on the platforms. Alex had played in that park many times before and he was always so timid on those high steps and steep slides. He never jumped around like the other kids.

Rob pictured his son's cautious steps and eventual glee as he flew down the metal slide. Tears welled in Rob's eyes, but sadness gave way to anger and he smashed his fist against the steering wheel over and over again. His hand slammed on the horn and it stopped the children and their parents in their tracks as they looked for the source of the sound.

Rob put the car in gear and left the playground to continue his futile search. Lane had gotten out of her truck as if to affirm her presence to him, but he rolled right past her. He drove by the house of the witness. There were still a couple of police cars outside and Rob slowed down a bit as he passed. The officer stationed outside the woman's door spoke into the walkie-talkie on his shoulder, his eyes fixed on Rob's car.

Though he had no idea where he was headed, Rob realized that his sweep of the neighborhood was a forlorn hope as he came to grips with the fact that his son was taken away and could be anywhere. He drove around, aimless and vagrant, with his FBI escort never quite out of sight and let the cold truth bite into his heart; Alex was gone. Simple and harsh.

He was just gone.

- 3 -

Marvin stared at the screen on the bank machine in despair. The balance had dwindled down to practically nothing. He withdrew twenty dollars and crumpled the receipt in his hand. Another friendly reminder of financial hardship.

The layoff had come at a most inopportune time. Though, there isn't ever a good time for losing your job for no reason. The severance pay had run out which meant bills and car loan payments had to take turns on who got paid each month. He thought things would be fine. They had a long-term plan, him and Darlene. But when the economy took a nosedive, middle management were the first victims squeezed out by the tightening of corporate belts.

The latest in vitro fertilization attempt had

failed and there was no way they could afford another round. They had started down that road when he was still back at his job. Benefits and prepayments and deposits were already paid and they couldn't back out of it all. Not that Darlene even wanted to. He sat in his truck and held the result letter, wondering how he would break the news to Darlene. She would be devastated again. He always worried about her when he had to leave for the odd jobs he picked up here and there. All alone in their country house with nothing to do but fritter and fret. He tried to convince her to get a job that she could go to a few days a week. Just something to distract her. He knew she could never keep a job very long, though, so he eventually let it go. It would always break his heart when she came home crying, jobless again. She simply wasn't cut out for the working world and they agreed that Marvin would provide. It was just as well; all she ever wanted was to be a mom. But that was just one more thing that he couldn't give her.

He started his truck and drove to his next job interview. He hoped it would be his last otherwise he'd have to expand out even further from home. They all said the same thing at the end: "We'll let you know."

Marvin waited his turn in a small room

with three other men who were there for the same job. He watched them all go in and leave until he was the only one left. The receptionist called him back and led him to a small office. He hoped his desperation wasn't obvious as he sat down across from the tired looking man on the other side of the desk. The man asked Marvin all the usual questions as he studied his résumé. The man leaned back in his chair and ran his hand across the strands of hair that covered his balding head.

"We're not a big operation here, Marv."

He hated it when people called him Marv. "You've clearly got a lot of experience driving trucks but for a company like ours, you'd have to use your own vehicle to make the deliveries."

"Sure. That's not a problem. My old clunker finally saw its last ride and now I've got a newer SUV," Marvin said.

"You'd be compensated for fuel, of course. Think your truck can handle a trip to DC and back three days a week?"

"Yes, sir."

"Well, Marv," the man said and nodded with his lips pulled tight. "I've got a good feeling about you. Can ya start Monday?"

Marvin smiled and breathed out in relief. He stood up and held out his hand to the man.

"Sure can. Thank you, sir."

"Call me Hank," he said and shook Marvin's hand. Hank had the receptionist take Marvin's information and bid him farewell. Marvin got back in his truck and relaxed for the first time since he was laid off from his old job. It wasn't much, but it was a paycheck.

His content relief gave way to tension as he looked at the envelope tucked in the visor. He still had to tell Darlene the bad news. This new job wouldn't pay enough to do another round of in vitro. It would only keep the bills paid until something with a better salary came along.

He took his time on the drive home and wondered if they should look at adoption.

He parked the truck at the end of the long driveway and readied himself to be the bearer of bad news. Darlene waited for him on the front porch. She waved when he got out and called out to him.

"How did it go?"

"Start Monday," he said with his arms out. They embraced and she whispered in his ear.

"That's great news, baby." The envelope crinkled in his hand and she pulled away. "What ya got there?"

"We should go inside."

He sat her down on the sofa and took the letter out. Her eyes were wide with expectation, as though he was about to hand her something wonderful. He watched her as she moved her lips and read. Her eager eyes slimmed and her mouth curled down with pure sadness. She blinked and two droplets landed on the page. Marvin moved closer to her and put his arms around her shoulders. She buried her head in his chest and sobbed. He saw her hand fall to the side as the tear-stained letter slipped from her fingers.

Marvin finally got back to work after Darlene's incident. Her wrists had long scarred over and though she had resumed her normal routines, he could sense the sadness that consumed her. He took her with him on his deliveries so she wouldn't be alone in the big old house with nothing to do. She would just look out the window, rubbing her scars as they rolled by the mountains. When Marvin would strike up a conversation, her responses were short and uninterested. He always did his best to steer clear of topics that would upset her. One of her only friends had just had a baby girl and he knew it would only hurt her to talk about it. She hadn't even spoken to the woman since they saw her at the market, her belly proudly pushed out and oblivious to Darlene's secret suffering.

As autumn approached, Darlene spent her days in their garden. It started as a small patch of dirt to grow a few vegetables, but she immersed herself and it expanded further and further. Marvin joined her on his days off and they worked the land together. She was more vocal while they toiled but, when the work was done, they would eat their dinner in distant silence. Marvin would read books on farming to try and keep up with her, hopeful that they could turn her hobby into something that could pay the bills. He mentioned it on one of their trips.

"Ya know, I've been reading up a bit. If we get serious, we could turn the farm into a real family business." He glanced between Darlene and the road. She stared out the window and ran her finger along the jagged scar as a tear rolled down her cheek.

"But we aren't even a real family..."

Marvin returned his gaze to the open road and said nothing more of it for the rest of their trip.

The days and weeks went by much the same. Darlene went on fewer road trips with him and Marvin worried about her every time he went out without her. He was terrified that she would try to take her own life again. Memories of that bloody night flashed in his mind as he drove and he struggled to push them out of his mind.

Then, one day, fear and worry melted away. Darlene was pregnant. The town physician confirmed it. Marvin thought it funny that once you completely give up on something, life has a way of dropping it right in your lap. Sometimes, the trials of heartache were a proving ground for future happiness. Darlene could barely contain her euphoria. Marvin had to convince her to at least wait until a few months had passed before she screamed it from the rooftops. Darlene hit all the expected conventions in those first few months. Weird cravings; nesting; swollen feet. Oh, those poor swollen feet. Marvin would massage them at night while she rubbed her belly, perfectly at peace with the universe. They would stay up far too late, coming up with names and playfully arguing about whether it was a boy or a girl. Money was tight, sure, but Marvin knew they could make it work. They were both more than ready to start a new chapter in their lives.

Their monthly appointment with the physician was typically a quick in and out. Just a formality to make sure everything was as it should be. Old-fashioned as he was,

Marvin sat in the waiting room during Darlene's examination. He flipped through an old Time magazine with an absent mind. The comings and goings of politicians and the plight of third world nations didn't interest him in the slightest. Darlene came out holding some papers in one hand and the other clutched at the collar of her dress. She was nervous. Anxious. Something was wrong. Marvin stood up and steadied her at the shoulders.

"What is it?"

Darlene shook her head, ever so slightly.

"We gotta go to county hospital," she said. Marvin fought away the million questions he had and led her out to the truck. As they drove, Darlene mumbled as she rubbed her belly.

"Ain't felt a kick in a couple days. Figured it weren't nothing."

Marvin sped up, mostly from nerves.

"What did the doctor day, Darlene?"

"Gotta go to county hospital. They got one of them ultrasound machines."

Marvin feared the worst as his eyes darted between the road and Darlene. She felt around her midsection as if searching for something.

He raced along the county roads and to the hospital. It was a blurred whirlwind once they arrived. Forms and requisitions. Questions that had to be repeatedly answered. Didn't anyone write their answers down? Everyone seemed to focus in on Darlene's scars. Marking wished they would let it be. Finally, the ultrasound technician called Darlene in. As always, Marvin waited. He waited and waited. He didn't bother with the even older magazines this time. He found an imperfection in the vinyl of the empty chair next to him and occupied himself by picking away at it. The chair across the way, though exactly the same, looked more comfortable and he switched spots. He counted the small butterflies that had been painted on the far wall. Seventy-four. A woman in scrubs came out from the back asked him to follow her. He was reluctant, but she said Darlene had asked for him.

The dark room was meant to be a calm, relaxing space. When he stepped inside, it was anything but. Darlene cried so hard she could barely catch a breath. Marvin stood at her side and rubbed her back.

"What is it?" he asked though deep down he already knew the answer. Darlene tried to tell him, but couldn't stop crying long enough to speak coherently. The ultrasound nurse took a chart with her as she left. She looked at Marvin and, before closing the door, let him know.

"I'm so sorry, sir. You lost the baby. Someone will be by in a few minutes to collect you."

And that was that. Short and frank. She closed the door and left them there to hold each other and cry.

The horrific ordeal went by like a blur for Marvin. They prepped Darlene like she was going in for surgery. Only it wasn't surgery. She had to deliver the baby.

A month later, Marvin made his last delivery in Alexandria and sat in his truck. Darlene had stayed home to tend her garden. She'd grown distant and quiet. He couldn't go on this way. Darlene wouldn't be able to get past never having children and he knew she would take her own life. He just knew it. She needed help they couldn't afford. She needed him to be home more. She needed companionship. She needed a child of her own. He had mentioned adoption a few times in the past, but they never pursued it for one reason or another.

Marvin cranked the engine and it sputtered to life. The long trips had taken their toll on his truck. They needed so many things and he simply couldn't get them. He drove along and the truck revved louder and louder. He managed to pull it into a gas station and topped off the fluids and oils. When he started it back up, it sounded much smoother. He knew a weekend of repairs awaited him. Marvin had to find his way back to the highway and drove slowly through the city streets. He didn't go to Alexandria often and was quickly disoriented. He pulled over in a quiet neighborhood and tried to get a grip on his bearings. He rummaged through the glove box and pulled out an old map book. He squinted as he tried to read the small street sign and found it on the map.

Before he pulled away, he leaned his head back in despair. No adoption agency would give a child to a part-time delivery man with a suicidal wife. Bless her heart, Darlene would be naive enough to tell them it was proof of just how much she wanted to be a mom. Marvin leaned his head against his hands on the steering wheel and cried. He knew it was only a matter of time before he lost Darlene and it would be his fault because he couldn't make her a mommy.

Marvin pulled himself together and was about to drive off. He saw a young boy in a red jacket walking slowly, with no real purpose. As he neared, Marvin saw fear and confusion in his face. There were no adults near him. The boy was alone, lost perhaps, but alone. He got out of his truck and the boy stopped when he saw him. Marvin knelt down and looked in the boy's teary eyes.

"You lost, big fella?"

The boy nodded. Marvin felt a twinge in his gut and, in that second, he made a decision that he could never go back on. He snatched the boy up and sensed pure fear as he hurried him inside the vehicle. The boy was smart enough to know not to go with strangers, but scared enough to do as he was told. He sped away, heart racing, and looked back every couple seconds to the child in the back seat. Marvin's heavy breath pumped out with pure adrenaline. He got out of the city as quick as he could and finally spoke to the boy.

"I'm gonna take you to your mommy."

- 4 -

Rob finally slowed to a stop at the end of Alexander Street and watched the fading sunlight sparkle on the river. He got out of his car and stared off across the water. The Interstate bridge to his right hummed with early evening traffic and Agent Lane's SUV pulled up right behind his car.

"What were you thinking, Rob?" she said as she got out. He didn't move or respond to her and Lane placed a hand on his shoulder. "Mr. Marshall."

"They could have gone anywhere. Any direction. I'm never going to see him again, am I?" Rob said as he turned to Lane, his eyes focused on hers as he tried to gauge her reaction.

"You shouldn't have taken off like that,

Rob."

"I know. I knew I wouldn't find him. The second I saw Gina holding his jacket in that evidence bag, I knew." Lane put a hand on his shoulder.

"We should get back to the house in case they call," she said.

"They won't," Rob said as he turned his gaze back toward the Potomac. "They won't."

Rob dragged his feet back to his car and headed home with Agent Lane close behind him the whole way. Most of the reporters had left and there were fewer FBI vehicles parked on the street. Lane told him they went to set up shop at the police department. Rob opened the front door and, though his house still bustled with federal agents, it felt empty. Gina drank some coffee at the kitchen table with Agent Brown and didn't notice him right away. Rob looked around the living room. No cartoons on the TV. No toys on the floor. No laughter or tiny feet stomped down the hallway.

"Rob, where have you been?" Gina called from the kitchen.

"I'm sorry, Gina," Rob said as he joined her at the table. "I shouldn't have left you here."

"It's fine." Her standard response for when she was upset with him. He deserved it, of course. He was selfish to leave like that.

"Agent Brown kept me company," she said.

Rob got up and poured himself a cup of coffee and the three of them sat in silence as they waited for the phone to ring or to hear news from the police department. Rob clinked his fingernails against his coffee cup which drew a glare from his wife. He noticed her silent disapproval but didn't stop right away. When Gina cleared her throat, he finally ceded and placed his hands down on the table. Rob had long finished his coffee and felt time slow down as they waited for a phone call that he knew in his heart would never come. But they waited, vigilant and hopefully deluded, until the late hours of the night. Lane agreed to stay with them through the night and suggested they get some rest.

Rob laid his wife down and sat down on the edge of the bed. He knew he wouldn't sleep but if his body somehow won the battle, his nightmare would be waiting for him when he woke. Rob spent the night up and down, not sure if Gina was awake or not. He stood and stepped down the hall to look in Alex's room. He took a few slow steps toward the bed and stroked the pillow where Alex should have been. Rob picked it up and held it close, the smell of kids shampoo filling his nose and wondered where his little boy laid his head that night. He took the pillow back to his room and returned to his perch on the edge of the bed until the first hints of morning light crept in through the drapes.

Rob heard Gina roll over. Her eyes were red and swollen.

"Did you sleep, Rob?" she said.

"No. Did you?"

"I couldn't."

Rob nodded and put the pillow down between them. Gina ran her fingers across it just like he had and started to cry.

"Come on," Rob said, "we'll see if there's any news." Gina stopped off at the washroom to fix herself up and Rob greeted Agent Lane with a limp wave of his hand on his way to the kitchen. She got up off the couch and joined him.

"You guys get any sleep?" she said. Rob just shook his head to respond. "I figured as much," Lane said. Gina shuffled her feet across the floor and turned on the coffee maker.

"Any news?" Gina said. Rob hadn't asked because he already knew the answer. The only sound he heard all night was the occasional quiet conversation between the few remaining agents in the house. No phones rang, no messages came. There wasn't even any chatter on the police officer's radio.

"No, Gina. No news," Lane said. Gina breathed out through her nose, weary and enervated. Rob sensed a change in Lane's tone and pressed the issue.

"So what do we do now?" he said. Agent Lane's lips straightened out across her face, likely unsure how her suggestion would be received.

"I think we should all go down to the police station," she said. "We can forward your calls there and stay on top of the investigation." Rob looked at Gina and nodded as he put his hand on her shoulder. It was the best thing to do. They couldn't do anything at home. It was just an empty reminder of the horror they were in.

They got themselves cleaned up and walked to Lane's truck. No reporters had stayed the night so their exit was uninterrupted. Rob noticed some drapes move aside from onlookers in the houses across the street. As they drove westward, Gina's wide eyes darted around at the buildings and parking lots just Rob's had the day before. Rob placed his hand on her knee and she stopped to look at him. He shook his head to steer her attention away from the unnecessary stress of the search. He'd been there already and it wouldn't do her any good. She clasped his hand in hers and looked down for the rest of the ride. Rob stared out the window at nothing in particular. The buildings and trees shot by, breaks in the skyline opened up and closed as they drove, and at last they arrived.

"Gonna go in the back way," Lane said. "Press will be out front." Neither of them responded and Lane parked the truck.

Agent Brown opened the door for them and led them inside. The frenzied cacophony of noise hit Rob and, though nobody ceased their activities, all eyes were on the parents of the missing boy as Agent Brown took them to one of the vacant offices. There was a small couch in the against the wall that faced the desk. The only light in the room was from a dim lamp in the corner and what bled through the drawn blinds.

"Make yourselves comfortable," Lane said. "I'm going to check in and get an update." After Lane had gone, Rob paced around the small room.

"Make ourselves comfortable?" he said as he leaned his hands on the desk.

"Rob, please," Gina said.

"What?"

"Just come and sit with me."

"Sorry," he said. "It's just—"

"I know," Gina said and tapped her palm on

the cushion next to her. Rob groaned as he lowered his body down. He shut his eyes for a moment and though the hum of the chaotic precinct loomed just outside the door, he tuned everything out and focused on the calm sound of Gina's hand as it moved up and down against the fabric of his shirt. Her gentle touch and the soft yellow light in the corner of the room made his eyes grow heavy. That brief moment was interrupted by the sharp knock and immediate entrance of Brown and Lane. They brought a man in with them. A typical bureau man, head to toe. He looked more like an accountant than a field agent. The dark jacket and neutral tie, the plain white dress shirt, the unremarkable hair, and clean-shaven face were all forgettable and ordinary. If it weren't for his ID badge, Rob would have figured him as just another Washington commuter who got lost on his way to work.

"Mr. and Mrs. Marshall, my name is Kyle Bishop with the Behavioral Analysis Unit," he said as he shook their hands. "Due to the time sensitive situation, we're here to offer any help that the CARD team could use and I was hoping I could ask you some questions."

"Time sensitive?" Gina said. Bishop put his papers down on the desk and leaned against it.

"Yes, ma'am. The first forty-eight hours are critical in these cases."

"Uh, we've already spoken to the police and the FBI," Rob said.

"If it's alright, I have some different questions," Bishop said. "The smallest details can help in our investigation."

Rob and Gina both agreed and answered the very specific questions. Bishop asked them about their daily routines, their work, Alex's friends and their parents. Each question was more focused and specific than the last. He finished his long inquiry and thanked them before he returned to the madness outside the room. Rob peered through the blinds and watched Bishop consult with, presumably, the rest of his team. They all stood in front of a big map pinned to the wall. They placed pins on it and drew big circles while they nodded to each other with their hands on their chins. Rob let the opening in the blinds snap closed and sat back down. He put his arm around Gina and held her close in the dark, silent room.

Every now and then, Lane or Brown would come in with food and water for them but, for the most part, all they did was sit in that small office. Rob checked his watch and realized that it had been a full day since anyone had seen Alex. He remembered what Bishop had told them and he became very aware of the urgency they were now faced with. They hadn't made any progress in the first twenty-four hours. The press conference didn't get them any leads. Rob wondered if the story was even still getting airtime. If the agents had any information at all, they hadn't shared it yet. No updates; no big breaks; just nothing.

As the hours passed and the sun started to set, the clamor of the investigative team outside the door died down. Rob opened the door a crack and looked out. The BAU agents had left and Rob hoped it was to search or follow a trail of breadcrumbs. It was shift change for the officers and there was a brief swell of volume as they overlapped. Some stayed, but most went home. Home to their families, Rob guessed. As the evening sun gave way to night, Gina seemed to grow impatient and slammed her hands on the cushions before she pushed her way past Rob. She stormed out to the main room and screamed out at everyone.

"Somebody please tell me what's going on!" Her voice almost echoed as the officers stopped their busy work. Necks craned and bodies turned toward the source of the outburst. Agent Lane hurried over from one of the gatherings of officers when she saw Gina.

"Anybody," Gina yelled again. "Please!" Agent Lane ushered her back inside the office and shut the door while Gina sobbed. "Please..." Rob saw the strong woman he married break. Even her voice was broken. Not from the scream but from mental fatigue. She was always the problem solver at home. But in there, her little boy gone, she couldn't do a thing. Lane kneeled down in front of her and laid her hand on Gina's shoulder.

"I know this isn't easy," Lane said. Gina was infuriated.

"You don't know anything!" she shouted at Lane.

"Mrs. Marshall—"

"You don't know anything!" Gina yelled again. She broke out in hysteric tears as Rob sat down next to her and held her in his arms. "You don't know anything..." she said it over and over again as she rocked in Rob's arms. Lane backed away from Gina and didn't respond. Rob looked up at her and his pleading eyes asked the agent for some sort of explanation. Lane spun a desk chair around and sat in front of the Marshalls.

"Gina, I just got word that Agent Bishop

interviewed the witness and was able to get a good description of the man that that took Alex," Lane said.

"A man?" Gina sat up with renewed strength. "What man?"

"Bishop is on his way back with the witness to give the description to a sketch artist. If anybody knows him, we should get some leads."

As if on cue, Agent Bishop knocked on the door and called Lane out to the main room. When both agents had gone, Rob raised the blinds and looked out across the floor. An older woman, maybe in her sixties, sat in front of an easel as she moved her hands and touched her face to describe the features. She had a nervous look about her, understandable with all the commotion about.

Rob and Gina stood and watched in silence as the woman continued her animated description. Rob's stomach panged and tightened as they neared completion of the sketch. The artist tilted his head back to take in the finished product and, satisfied, he showed it to the woman. She nodded and pointed a bony finger as she looked at everyone who had gathered to see.

Bishop took the picture and scanned it at a computer before he walked toward Rob and his wife. Gina wrung her hands in anticipation and Rob felt his limbs tingle as he wiggled his fingers to shake the sensation.

Bishop entered with purpose and Rob hoped, as strange as it felt, that he would recognize the face on the paper. The day before, Agent Brown had mentioned some statistic about familiar faces. If Rob knew the face, they could find Alex and lock the sick bastard up.

"Mr. and Mrs. Marshall," Bishop said, "do you recognize this man?" Rob's heart sank and he felt himself weaken when Bishop turned the page over.

"No," Rob said as he sat down and rested his head against his palm. Gina studied it with extreme attention but her face relaxed and her stern focus changed to disappointment. She sat down and just shook her head. Rob could tell she had the same hope to recognize the man.

"We'll get this out to the press," Bishop said. "Somebody knows this guy." He left with the picture and gathered his team. Rob sat there, defeated and hopeless. Lane came back in and suggested they all go back to the house and get some rest. Dejected and sullen, they stood and followed the agent out the back door and got in her truck.

As they drove back home, Rob watched Gina stare out the window as her expression transformed from limp sadness to the downturned lips and flared nostrils of anger. Rob touched her arm to console her. Gina snapped it away and hissed a whisper through her teeth.

"This is your fault."

- 5 -

"What the hell are you talking about?" Rob noticed Agent Lane turn an ear toward the back seat.

"This is all your fault." Gina seethed as she held her gaze out the window.

"Gina, do you hear yourself?" Rob said. "Look, I know you're upset but—"

"Upset?" she screamed at him. "My son has been kidnapped and we can't find him. Yes, I'm upset, Rob." Just as he was about to explode at his wife, Agent Lane interjected.

"Guys, don't do this to each other," she said. "This isn't anyone's fault, do you hear me?" Rob and Gina didn't say anything to respond, but the tension in the vehicle was almost tangible. "You guys need to be strong right now and turning on each other won't help anything." Lane spoke as though she'd said it a million times. Gina turned her head away and resumed her cold stare out the window.

"This never would have happened if we sent him to Ryerson," she said under her breath, but still loud enough for Rob to hear. He chose not to fuel the fire and didn't say a word. They spent the rest of the ride in silence and Rob retreated to his computer room so he could check his e-mail. Gina huffed out a frustrated sigh as he disappeared down the hall.

Rob had hundreds of messages and only opened the one from his boss. He had seen everything on TV and told Rob to take all the time off he needed. In the darkened room, the electric glow of the computer screen burned Rob's tired eyes. He rested his head on his palms to shield the light and be alone with his frantic, racing thoughts. Try as he might he couldn't focus on any one thing. He endured flashing memories of Alex smiling, laughing, and crying. He wondered if he was cold; his jacket was down at the police station. He hoped whoever had him was taking care of his little man. He tried to fight the torturous thoughts of Alex scared or hurt. Or worse. Rob shook his head in his hands. Maybe Gina was right. If he hadn't insisted on a public school to save a few lousy bucks, they'd be sitting down for dinner as a family. Instead, their lives were torn apart and nothing else seemed to matter. Work. Money. All the trivial, pointless fights. Nothing.

After an hour alone, Rob went to the kitchen and ate some fruit while Gina sat at the table. Agent Lane looked over some paperwork on the couch. Rob could tell that the investigation wouldn't get them anywhere. He felt it in his very being. The authorities were winding down and would have to focus their efforts on new cases. Bishop's words echoed in his mind. *The first forty-eight hours are critical.* Time burned away too fast and Rob knew that meant the likelihood of getting Alex back lessened with each passing hour. Rob paced the hallways and rooms of the house as the clocks on the walls taunted him and clicked the seconds into history. Every half hour, Lane called someone to check in for news.

"Keep me posted," she said at the end of each call. Rob wandered back and forth through the house and drew the glare of Gina when he passed by the entrance to the kitchen. She just sat there, her coffee mug clutched in her grasp. Rob knew that her earlier outburst was just nerves and frustration, but he couldn't quite forgive her for it yet, however displaced it was. Lane's phone rang and Rob stopped in his tracks at the sound. Lane nodded along as she listened to the caller and responded with a simple yes or no every few seconds. Gina had straightened up in her seat and waited for Lane to finish before she came out to the living room. Lane hung up and took a deep breath before she addressed them.

"Anything?" Gina said.

"Too early to tell, but the teams are checking out a few leads. They hit a few dead ends, but it's something," Lane said. Gina lowered her shoulders and returned to the kitchen to slump back in her chair again. Hours went by with no sound in the house but Rob's pacing footsteps and Lane's periodic phone call to check in. In the small hours of the morning, Lane called in less. Every hour or so. Agent Brown came back just before sunrise and brought breakfast for everyone. She sent Lane to the station and posted herself at the front door of the house.

The morning passed by without any developments. Rob saw a single news van stop in front of the house and the reporter spoke to the camera for a minute or two before they packed up and left. A quick clip to air between segments. Alex had become a filler piece for the media. They'd move on to the next big scoop once the investigation lost its momentum. Maybe a few updates here and there but, for the most part, a forgotten story. Rob ate some lunch with Gina. The food was tasteless and served as simple fuel to keep him awake. Gina had finished and looked at her watch with tears in her eyes. Rob checked the time and realized that it had been two full days since anyone had seen Alex. Gina must have thought the same thing and remembered what Agent Bishop had said.

"They're only statistics, you know," Brown said from the front door. Rob almost forgot that she was there. She hadn't even turned around. "All that stuff you hear on TV shows; after forty-eight hours, the survival rate lowers or the case goes cold. It's all just statistics. Statistics and guesses. Nobody knows for sure." Rob walked out to the living room and sat on the arm of the couch.

"Agent Brown?" he said. She rubbed her string bracelet between her thumb and finger as she stared out the small window in the front door and turned to Rob as if snapped out of a daydream. "Can I ask how long they had your boy before they found him?" Brown clutched her hand over the keepsake and straightened her sleeve to conceal it.

"They didn't find him," she said. "He might still be out there. He might not." Rob noticed that Gina had joined them in the living room and Brown continued. "Like I said, they're just statistics. Every case is different."

"I'm sorry," Rob said. "I didn't mean to pry." Brown dismissed it with a wave of her hand and set her distant stare back out the tiny window.

"Is that why you joined the FBI?" Gina said. Brown nodded and looked over to them.

"There's always hope," she said with a slight smile to assure them but, likely, herself as well. Gina put her arm around Rob. In a cold shoulder argument, affection was always her initial form of apology and Rob showed silent forgiveness with a gentle touch on her hand as he let himself fall into her embrace.

An hour later, Rob stirred awake. He and Gina had fallen asleep on the couch, exhausted from the ordeal. He had slept long enough to dream and his waking mind hoped it had all been a horrible nightmare. Once his vision cleared, he saw Lane and Brown at the entrance of the house and fantasy gave way to reality. Rob didn't catch the start of their conversation and he could only just make out their hushed voices.

"The higher-ups are giving us until the end of the day," Lane said.

"Figured that was coming soon," Brown said. "Bishop have any luck?" Lane pulled her lips against her teeth and shook her head.

"He recommended getting the story to go national on the news, but no, all the leads were dead ends."

"Too bad. I'll let them know when they wake up."

"I'm up," Rob said to announce himself. Brown, surprised, turned to face him.

"Mr. Marshall, you have to understand—"

"You don't have to do that," he interrupted. "I know how it is. No leads, no breaks. Your team is needed elsewhere." He patted Gina's thigh to wake her up. She groaned in protest, but he shook her leg and got in a slight jab. "Come on, honey. Say goodbye to the FBI agents." Gina woke with a confused look on her face as she rubbed her eyes.

"What are you talking about?" she said. "What about Alex?"

"We aren't leaving just yet, Mrs. Marshall," Brown said.

"But we will have to go later tonight," Lane said as she fished a business card out of her back pocket. "Alexandria PD will take over the investigation, but if you need anything from us, don't hesitate to call me." Lane headed back outside and drove off. Brown stayed posted at the front door. Rob knew that they couldn't count on the authorities to do much more for them and Gina's demeanor seemed to reflect his as she checked her watch.

"Come on, Rob. It's getting late. Let's get something to eat," she said. They went to the kitchen and Brown didn't move. After Rob and Gina finished their meal, Brown stepped outside and came back in with a man in a beige trench coat. Rob figured he was a cop, but he had the look of a seasoned detective, right down to the scruffy mustache and the cheap shirt and tie combination under his coat. The man spoke with Brown for a few minutes. His voice was hushed and his eyes darted around the house as he wrote on a small notepad. He ran his thumb and forefinger across the hair on his upper lip as the agent spoke to him. After their short conversation, Brown introduced the man.

"Guys, this is Detective Hillman," she said. "He's going to take over the investigation." She tightened her lips and curled a small smile as she looked at Rob and Gina one last time. They all watched her leave and the detective huffed out a breath to pull attention his way. He took out his small notepad again and tapped his pen against the page like he couldn't decipher his own words.

"Mr. and Mrs. Marshall," Hillman said, "I have some questions for you. Just need to fill in a few blanks is all."

"Of course," Rob said.

"So Mr. Marshall, you were at work when your wife called you?"

"Yes."

"You're in marketing, right?" Hillman said as he checked his notepad.

"That's right. Why is that important?"

"Ah, my Captain always tells me I'm too thorough," Hillman said.

"No, it's fine," Rob said.

"Rob works at the top marketing firm in the area," Gina said. "Just got a nice promotion, too."

"Well, isn't that something?" Hillman said with false enthusiasm. "Sure would be a lot of folks after a spot like that, wouldn't there?"

"Oh my, yes," Gina said. "But my Rob is a real go-getter."

"Is that so, Mr. Marshall?" Rob didn't care for the condescension in the detective's voice and sensed an air of suspicion in his questions.

"What are you getting at, Detective?" Rob

said.

"Oh geez. I'm doing it again, aren't I?"

"Rob, please. The man only asked you about your job," Gina said. Hillman smiled his manipulative grin at Gina and his lips flattened when he looked at Rob.

"Anybody in the office who might have taken offense to a young go-getter like you snagging that sweet gig?"

"Maybe," Rob said as he shrugged his shoulders.

"I guess they probably wouldn't tell you flat out anyhow." Hillman chuckled a little. "I mean, who would say a thing like that?"

"Right," Rob said.

"And what about you, ma'am? You were here at home when the school called?"

"That's right. Now that Alex is in school all day, I'm taking some online courses for accounting." Gina seemed relieved to talk about mundane things. Rob, however, felt like Hillman was trying to lull her into incrimination as his fake smile grew bigger.

"There's something I'm not too clear on," Hillman said as he rubbed the hair above his lip. "Mr. Marshall, you left for a period of time at the beginning of the investigation."

"Yes."

"Where'd you go?"

"To look for Alex."

"Why?" Hillman said. Rob grew impatient with the detective.

"Don't know if you heard, but he's missing."

"But you didn't tell anyone you were leaving?"

"They said I should stay."

"And you left anyway?" Hillman shrugged his shoulders as he turned to Gina. "Seems strange."

"You've got some nerve, Detective. I'm not gonna sit here and let you accuse me of—."

"Rob, please," Gina interrupted. "He's just doing his job."

"It's quite alright, Mrs. Marshall. I'm just trying to understand," Hillman said. Rob stood up, enraged by the interrogation disguised as fact-finding.

"Understand? I hope you never really do understand what we're going through." Rob stormed out of the kitchen and didn't bother to lower his voice as he left. "Son of a bitch."

Rob sat on the edge of his son's bed and held his head in his hands. From Alex's room, Rob could hear Detective Hillman's voice as he continued his interview with Gina.

"Your husband seems a little short-tempered," Hillman said.

"Oh, you'll have to forgive Rob. This whole thing has just been so..." Gina's voice trailed off.

"Not a problem, Mrs. Marshall. Is Rob usually quick to temper?"

"No more than anyone else, I guess."

"I see. How about taking off? Is that typical?"

"Sometimes," Gina said.

"How are things between you two?"

"You know how it is, Detective," Gina said. "We have fights here and there."

"And how is he with Alex?" Hillman said.

"Great."

"Does he ever lose his temper around the boy?"

"What do you mean, Detective?" Hillman's voice lowered as if he leaned in to share a secret.

"Has he ever hurt Alex before?"

"Goodness, no," Gina said. "Rob would never—"

"Standard questions, ma'am." Hillman interrupted. "Ya know, I think I've got everything I need for tonight. You've been a big help, Mrs. Marshall."

"Anytime, Detective."

"You'll be seeing more of me, but I really should be going now." Rob listened as the heels of Hillman's cheap dress shoes clicked across the hardwood floor. The door opened and closed and Rob peeked out the window to watch Hillman slog himself across the lawn to talk to a uniformed officer who was parked on the street. Rob couldn't hear them, but could tell from the jerks of Hillman's head and pointing toward the house that the detective had a suspect list with just one name on it.

Rob Marshall.

- 6 -

Gina leaned against the door frame of Alex's room, her arms folded.

"Rob, I know this is tough, but Detective Hillman is just trying to help," she said.

"Don't be so naive, Gina," Rob said. "He's trying to pin this on us. On me."

"You're being ridiculous."

"We'll see," Rob said.

"Why don't we get some sleep?" Gina moved her head toward their bedroom. Rob closed the curtain over and heard Hillman's car pull away as they laid down. Gina nestled herself against Rob and was asleep within minutes. Rob stared at the dark ceiling and replayed the past few days in his head. His closed his weary eyes and drifted off to sleep. Every creak of the house or strong wind made Rob shoot awake throughout the night and look across the hall. From their room, he could always hear Alex's heavy breath in the night. But there was no sound from across the hall.

When the morning light crept through a small opening in the curtains, Gina stirred and Rob woke again. He had slept some but didn't feel any more alert. Gina went to the kitchen and made breakfast while Rob got dressed. When he joined her, she was staring into the fridge with an absent look on her face.

"You alright, honey?" Rob said. Gina just gazed at the shelves. Rob touched her shoulder to grab her attention. "Gina," he said to rouse her.

"We need milk, Rob." Her voice was distant and flat. "Alex likes milk. I want to make sure we have some for when he comes back."

"Honey..." Rob didn't want to upset her so he held his tongue. "I'll go and get some after breakfast." Gina smiled at him and went about her morning rituals. Rob checked on Gina after he ate. She studied one of her textbooks on the couch and Rob jingled his car keys to tell her that he was leaving. She smiled at him again.

"Thanks, honey," Gina said and turned her attention back to her book.

Rob shook his head at his wife's denial and

left. When he got in his car, he understood why she acted that way, though. He was off to get some milk. An utterly mundane errand but it felt just a little bit better to take his mind off of everything. He drove off and listened to the sound of the tires hum against the road.

Without realizing, he went in the opposite direction of Alex's school even though there was a grocery store nearby. A few extra minutes didn't seem like a big deal. The streets weren't very busy since rush hour had passed and Rob noticed a beige car in his rear view mirror. It was far enough back that he couldn't make out the driver, but it had been behind him for a few blocks. Paranoia made him take an unplanned turn on a side street and the beige car followed. He slowed his speed and so did his follower. He sped up and the beige car did the same. Rob still couldn't see the driver so he turned at every corner to try and shake him, barely slowing down at the stop signs until he reached a grocery store. Instead of parking out front he went around the back to the loading docks and parked next to a big delivery truck. He got out and leaned against his car to wait for his pursuer. The beige car sped past him and slammed the brakes hard. Detective Hillman hoisted himself out of the driver's seat and didn't bother to close the door behind him.

"Looking for me, Detective?" Rob called to him.

"What the hell are you doing?" Hillman said as he huffed his way over to Rob.

"We're out of milk."

"You think this is some kind of joke?"

"Why are you following me, Detective?"

"Now listen here, Mr. Marshall—"

"No, you listen! I don't know what you've got against me but instead of following me around you should be doing your job and looking for my son."

"I am doing my job," Hillman said. The smug look on his face dripped with condescension.

"How?" Rob said with his arms spread wide. Hillman's face was red and his lips were turned down in anger.

"I think you're hiding something. You were at the school pretty quick. You disappear in the middle of an investigation to God knows where. Driving around like a maniac. You've got a short fuse, too. I think you know something. I think you're behind this whole thing." Rob's bottled emotion boiled over as he felt his fist fly at the Detective's mouth and he planted it right on his stupid mustache. Hillman stumbled backward and held his hand to his face. He checked his palm for blood and spat on the ground as he pulled handcuffs out of his coat. Rob was shocked that he actually punched a cop and knew it was a huge mistake. Hillman grabbed his forearm and yanked Rob's arms behind him as the handcuffs clicked around his wrists.

"Alright, tough guy," Hillman said as he turned Rob toward the beige car. "Let's go for a little ride." Rob's head almost hit the door frame as Hillman hurried him into the back seat and slammed the door shut. The detective stood outside and wrote in his notepad for a couple minutes. Then he just stood there with his back to Rob and his hands on his waist, motionless as he basked in pride. When Hillman got in the car, Rob could see his round face in the big rear view mirror. His mouth twisted up in smug satisfaction as he turned the engine over. Hillman glanced back at Rob every now and then but drove in silence to the police station.

When they arrived, there was a lone white van in front of the station. A reporter spoke to a camera and stopped when she saw Rob in the back seat of Hillman's car. She pointed to get the cameraman's attention and he swung around, his lens fixed on Rob as

Hillman dragged him out.

"Are you getting this?" the reporter said as Hillman led Rob inside. All of the officers inside fell silent and watched Hillman take Rob to an interrogation room with glass walls. Hillman fished around in his pockets and found the handcuff keys.

"Sit down a minute," he said. "I'll be right back." Rob rubbed his red wrists. Handcuffs didn't feel like he thought they would. They really dug into his bones. Maybe in the excitement Hillman put them on too tight. Rob watched through the glass as Hillman spoke with a man who looked stressed out and frustrated with the detective. Hillman seemed to try and reason with the man and pointed back toward Rob while he spoke. The man shook his head like he was trying to hold back an outburst and held his hand out to Hillman. The detective gave him his little black notebook. He flipped through it, eyes up and down between the scribbles and Hillman. When the man finished, he tapped the notebook against his palm and pointed down a hallway to dismiss Detective Hillman. Rob smiled as he watched him shuffle away.

The stressed out man went back in his office and closed the door. After a few minutes, he came back out with a file in hand and stomped over to the glass room. An officer swiped a card and unlocked the room to let him in. He set the file down on the table and took a the chair on the other side of the table.

"Mr. Marshall, I'm Captain Roger Milton." His voice was drained and worn. Rob just wanted to go home and steered the conversation.

"Any news on my son?" he said. Milton lifted his head and furrowed his brow as if Rob had spoken in a foreign tongue. "That's why what's-his-face brought me here, isn't it? I mean, why else would he drag me down to the police station?" Rob emitted sarcastic disdain for Hillman, but the captain was not amused.

"Mr. Marshall," he said, his voice was more official and imposing. "You assaulted a police officer. Do you realize how serious that is?" Rob nodded but didn't change his expression. He wouldn't hesitate to punch Hillman again if he had the chance. The whole thing left a sour taste in his mouth for Alexandria PD and he knew he couldn't count on them to find Alex.

"So nothing new?" Rob said. Milton opened the file and flipped through the pages of reports.

"I want you to know we're going to follow

any leads we get, Mr. Marshall." Rob volleyed the magic words that would let him walk out the front door.

"Does that mean Hillman will stop harassing me and start looking for Alex?" Milton closed the file and gestured to the glass door.

"Your car is out front on a tow truck, Mr. Marshall." Rob stood up. The officer outside the door gave Milton an asking glance and the captain waved his hand to tell him to unlock it. Rob stepped out and saw Hillman peek around the corner from down the long hallway at him. Milton followed behind Rob as he walked and stopped him at the front door.

"Rob," he said. "Listen, we won't give up, but I've been around long enough to know how these things usually turn out. Do yourself a favor, try to move on." Rob lowered his head and sighed.

"That sounds an awful lot like giving up, Captain."

"Call me directly if you want to check on the case." Milton held out his business card and Rob put it in his back pocket. Hillman bounded over from his hiding spot and confronted Milton.

"You're letting him go?"

"Back off, Hillman," Milton commanded.

"We're not gonna have any more trouble here are we, Detective?" Hillman pulled his lips back against his teeth and gave in.

"No, sir," he said and his flared nostrils relaxed.

"No hard feelings?" Rob said as he pressed his own fist against his jaw. Hillman suppressed his obvious rage and shook his head. Milton, satisfied, headed back toward his office. "Oh good," Rob said. "I like cops. Always wanted to be a cop." Hillman smiled at him through gritted teeth. "But then I found out my parents were married when I was born so, that was that." Hillman straightened his posture and puffed up his chest. Even Rob was surprised at his own audacity and he turned to the door and stepped outside. The reporter and her cameraman were still there and a newspaper photographer had joined them. Rob walked past them as the camera clicked and the reporter scrambled to keep up with him. She held her microphone in front of him as he walked.

"Mr. Marshall, why did police bring you in for questioning?"

"No comment."

"You were in handcuffs, though. Are you a suspect?"

"Just a misunderstanding."

Rob got in his car as the reporter threw her arms up in frustration. He headed home and almost forgot to stop at the grocery store.

When he got home, Gina was busy at the computer with her studies.

"Did you remember the milk?" she called out.

"Got it," he said.

"What took you so long?"

"Just stopped at the police station on the way."

"Anything new?"

"Nope," Rob lied. He didn't want to worry Gina. He started to think that Captain Milton might be right. Gina seemed to be in a state of blissful ignorance, but he just couldn't switch off the obsession. The police were out of leads, the FBI was off the case, and his wife was delusional and thought Alex would just show up one day. Rob put the container of milk in the fridge and saw a picture on the carton that he hadn't noticed in the store. It was a missing child. A girl who had been missing for three years. Rob had never paid any attention to those pictures before. He wondered how many other people were the same way. If Alex was the child in the picture, how many people would even give it a second look?

- 7 -

Marvin spent his days in a paranoid frenzy. He imposed insane rules on Darlene, but she was so happy to care for the boy that she went along with all of it. They had never watched much television to begin with, but Marvin had disconnected the antenna so that Darlene wouldn't see the news. He told her that TV would rot the boy's brain. He told her that regular school would be too much for him to handle so she had to homeschool him. She didn't even question his bogus adoption story. She was simply overjoyed that she finally had a child of her own. He told her that his name was Mikey. It was her favorite name for a boy and the one they had picked out when they were doing in vitro. She was thrilled. He concocted a story that all the boys at the foster home would pretend to have different names. Darlene bought into it even when he cried and cried that his name was Alex. Boys will be boys.

For the first few days, the boy was a wreck. A steady stream of tears and outbursts as he cried out for his family. Marvin would take him outside behind the tall corn stalks, away from Darlene, to make the boy understand.

"You need to behave yourself, Mikey," he said. Little Alex Marshall just wouldn't let his old life go and stomped his feet in frustration.

"My name isn't Mikey! Stop calling me that!"

"You will behave, Mikey. I never want to hear you talk about the city again. This is your home now. We are your family. Do I make myself clear?"

Marvin towered over the cowering boy. He had to take a firm approach, just like his father had with him. Stern, feared, and respected, but fatherly all at once. It was a fine line to walk and he realized it was not as easy or natural as his old man made it look back then. It was especially difficult in their delicate situation. Marvin needed to repeat himself many times in the beginning. Each time he sensed himself showing more and more frustration, but it worked. Darlene could never know the truth and Marvin made sure that Mikey feared him just enough to hush up about it all. Stern, feared, and respected. Fatherly would have to wait.

Marvin kept close to home for the first couple of weeks, barely even going out for errands. He convinced Darlene that people would be jealous of their family and might try to take Mikey away. Eventually, the crying lessened and the boy seemed to accept his new home and family. There was an occasional outburst, but he always stopped when Marvin took him out behind the tall stalks of corn.

He told Darlene that Mikey had grown attached to his foster family and it would just take time for him to break out of it. He convinced Darlene of all these things and tried to convince himself as well.

They could give him a nice life here. Away from the big city. He could teach the boy honest, hard work on their little farm. He would be better off there. He would be happier in time. He wouldn't have to grow up in a cesspool like the DC area with all the cheating liars who took everything they had for granted. He had rescued the boy from an awful existence.

In the quiet evenings, the sounds of

emergency vehicles could be heard all the way from the highway. Marvin would stare out the window, his gun tucked in the back of his pants, making sure nobody came to his house.

Darlene had Mikey help her in the ever-expanding garden. Eventually, Marvin sensed a change in the boy as the months passed by. The anxiety waned. He settled into their daily routines. The sadness and dejection in his eyes were gone. He would beam with pride when they made something for dinner with food that he had grown. If things kept on, Marvin could stop doing deliveries and start their family farm one day. Mikey's drawings hung on the fridge with magnets. Darlene smiled at them every time she passed by them. Their marriage was never stronger. Their house was a now a home. They were a real family. And, at long last, Mikey finally called them mommy and daddy. Marvin felt that, deep down, they were just labels the boy used to identify them. It didn't go unnoticed by Darlene, though. He saw a happiness in her eyes that first time he said mommy. He couldn't even describe it if he wanted to.

They were finally a real family.

- 8 -

Rob finished another long day at work. He took any project that he could get his hands on and buried himself in long hours at the office. He usually spent at least ten hours a day at the office. His bosses tried to get him to slow down a bit because his pace made them look bad. Rob just kept going, though, without a care for outside perception. Even as everyone booked vacation time for Christmas, he didn't slow down. He couldn't bear to be at home during the holidays without Alex.

Snow had fallen in the afternoon and the plows hadn't come out so the roads were nice and empty for his ride home. When he got there, the house was dark. Gina never remembered to turn the porch light for him.

He didn't see the light from the television either. Gina was probably on the computer as usual. Rob opened the door and flicked the lights on.

"I'm home," he called out.

"Dinner's on the stove," Gina said from the office. Rob took off his coat and went in the kitchen. There was a pot of spaghetti on the burner and a jar of sauce on the counter. It had all gone cold so he popped some in the microwave and ate alone at the small kitchen table. After dinner, Rob watched the sports highlights and Gina finally emerged.

"I'm going to bed," she said.

"K."

"Don't forget we have group tomorrow night."

"Yep." Rob didn't look away from the television and Gina huffed as she turned around. After a few hours of channel surfing and some mindless reality shows, Rob dozed off and slept on the couch.

The next evening, they drove down to the community center. The roads were busy with holiday shoppers who zoomed around to get last minute deals.

"I wonder how many people will even be there tonight," Gina said. Rob nodded and kept his eyes on the road. "So how's work going?" Rob was caught off guard at Gina's attempt at small talk.

"Work is work," he said. "Fine, I guess."

"Busy?"

"Yeah. It's that time of year. Everyone taking time off."

"Oh, I almost forgot. Your secretary called the house last night."

"Executive assistant," Rob said.

"What?"

"Amanda is my executive assistant. They're not called secretaries anymore, Gina."

"Anyway, she said your meeting is canceled on Monday morning."

"Oh," Rob said.

"She sounds nice." Gina straightened in her seat.

"I guess she is." Rob was still thrown off by the chit-chat, but they had arrived at the community center and headed inside. There was still a good number of people in attendance despite how close it was to Christmas. Rob and Gina took their usual chairs just like everyone else did and a few minutes later, the meeting started. There was a new couple there and they shared their story. Their daughter had committed suicide a few years back. Rob didn't feel much of a connection with any of the other parents. Of course he felt for them, but at least they all knew where their kids were.

Rob didn't even know if Alex was alive. Gina read somewhere that the Surviving Parents group might help them cope, but Rob just couldn't give himself over to the whole thing. He couldn't act like Alex was dead and try to move on.

Rob listened with an absent ear as the others spoke. He shook his head when the facilitator asked if he had anything to share. The only single person there, Derek, finished with a story about some sort of yearly ritual. Rob didn't really pay attention to him.

They took a break and Rob headed straight to the free coffee while some of the others mingled. As he dumped in his sugar and cream, he noticed Gina talking to Derek. She had to crane her neck to look up at him. Rob stirred his coffee and watched them. Gina's finger twirled a strand of hair and she smiled at him while he spoke. He must have told a funny story because Gina laughed and touched his chest. Rob tossed his stir stick and walked over to them. He jutted his chin up at Derek.

"Hey, Rob. Good to see you," Derek said and smiled.

"Derek," Rob said and touched Gina on the shoulder. "Can I talk to you for a second, Gina?"

"Rob, I'm having a conversation with

Derek. Don't be rude."

"It's OK," Derek said. "I was just gonna grab some coffee before we start again." Rob took Gina by the arm to a quiet corner of the room.

"What the hell is wrong with you, Rob?"

"Me? You flirt with another guy and ask me what's wrong?"

"You're imagining things, Rob. We were just talking."

"Oh sure," Rob said. "Twirling your hair, touching him, pushing your chest out. Yeah, just talking. You think I didn't see that?"

"I'm surprised you even noticed me, Rob," Gina said as she crossed her arms. "You and your secretary, sorry, *executive assistant*, being so busy lately."

"What does Amanda have to do with anything?"

"Oh please, Rob. Long hours, late nights, and a new secretary. I'm not stupid, you know."

"Now who's imagining things?"

Derek sauntered over toward them and Rob jerked his head with a glare of contempt. Derek stopped in his tracks and headed to his seat. Rob looked back at Gina and her lips were twisted up in a smirk.

"Maybe if you paid any attention to me I wouldn't feel like I had to go to such lengths,

Rob." She strolled back to her seat and swayed her hips from side to side as she passed in front of Derek. Rob took a deep breath through his flared nostrils as he watched her shameless taunt.

Rob spent the rest of the meeting hunched forward in his chair and didn't look at Gina. They drove home in complete silence. Rob felt Gina look at him every now and then, but he just listened to the sound of the wet snow as it sloshed against the tires. When they got home, Rob flopped on the couch and turned on the TV to watch the end of the hockey game. Gina huffed in disapproval and, as she headed down the hallway, voiced her frustration.

"Unbelievable," she said and slammed a door. After the game, Rob dozed off and slept on the couch. Again.

Rob woke up to a sizzling sound from the kitchen and a metal pan clanged as Gina pulled it down from its perch. The smell of breakfast filled his nose. Rob groaned as he sat up and stretched. Gina heard him and poked her around the corner.

"I was wondering when you'd get up," she said. Rob rubbed his eyes and adjusted to the morning as he shuffled his feet to the kitchen.

"What's all this?" he said.

"Sunday breakfast. Just like we used to do."

"Hmm," Rob said. He went to the bathroom and came back to a plate waiting for him. They are together but didn't speak except to comment on the food. When Rob finally finished, Gina took his plate to the sink and turned to face him, her hands propping her up on the counter.

"About last night," Gina said.

"Forget it," Rob said. "I already have." Gina nodded and smiled, but had an air of anxiety about her. She fidgeted and didn't seem sure of what to do with her hands. Rob got changed out of his old clothes and decided to head to the gym. As he put on his running shoes, Gina stopped him.

"You're leaving?" she said.

"Yeah. Gonna lift some weights. I won't be long."

"But—"

"What is it, Gina?"

"I want to have another baby."

"What?" Rob said. He was blindsided. "You want to have another baby?"

"Yes, Rob," Gina said. "I want another baby."

"You can't be serious."

"I am," she said. Rob stood at the doorway, his mouth open, unable to speak. "Just think about it," Gina said. "We'll talk later when you get back." She turned and resumed her tidying in the kitchen. Rob stayed frozen at the front door. Mere hours before, Gina taunted him in misguided jealousy and then, out of nowhere, a big breakfast and a proposal like that.

"Have a good workout," Gina called out from the kitchen.

"Yeah," Rob said as he grabbed his keys from the hook. "See ya soon." As he drove, he tried to process what Gina said. He figured if he gave her some time she would realize it was a bad idea and she would let it go. He put it out of his mind while he worked out. Rob pushed himself hard at the gym and burned off the frustration of the previous night.

He threw his gym bag in the car and grabbed some eggnog from the grocery store in the plaza. On the way home, he stopped at the liquor store for some rum. Since his meeting was canceled, he didn't have to be up and at it early in the morning.

When Rob got home, Gina's car was gone. He went in and found a note on the TV. She went out shopping with her girlfriends. Rob had a shower and made himself a nice eggnog drink. He channel surfed for a while and refilled his glass. After a few hours, Gina still wasn't home. Rob wasn't surprised, though. When they got going, there was no stopping them. Rob felt hungry and couldn't find anything he wanted in the house so he decided to go to over to the sports bar for a burger. It wasn't far away so he figured he would be fine to drive. He watched the football game while he ate and had a few beers before he headed back home.

Gina's car was in the driveway but, as usual, the lights were off. When he went in, he saw red rose petals strewn about on the floor. A soft glow of candlelight flickered from down the hallway and the scent of vanilla filled his nose. He sighed and guessed that he hadn't been clear enough earlier about having another baby. He wasn't ready. He didn't think she was ready, either. She had been too up and down over the past few months. It was too soon. Even nine months later would be too soon. He just wasn't ready. Rob threw his bag on the table and looked on the bright side. At least they could officially make up for the night before.

"Gina, I'm home," he called out. She didn't answer and he took his shoes off. He followed the trail of rose petals toward the candlelight. It came from the bathroom. "Gina?" he said as he turned the corner. Still no answer. He peeked his head in the doorway. It was dark except for the yellow glow of the flame and Gina was in the tub with her eyes closed. As Rob's eyes adjusted to the light, he noticed she was wearing a nightgown and the water was a light, translucent red.

"Gina?" he said as he inched closer. Rob saw that the water wasn't red from the rose petals. It was the threads of blood that billowed out from the long gashes on her wrists.

- 9 -

Rob ran alongside the stretcher as the paramedics rushed through the wide doors in the hospital hallways. At the end of the long hall, he was stopped by a woman in scrubs.

"You can't come in here, sir."

"She's my wife," Rob said.

"You'll have to wait over there." She pointed to a small alcove and a line of chairs against the wall. "We'll keep you informed," she said and disappeared behind the closing doors.

Rob sat hunched forward in the chair, his head in his hands. He waited for what felt like hours as he alternated pacing back and forth and sitting. Finally, the woman in scrubs came into the small waiting area.

"Sir, your wife is going to be fine," she said.

"Oh, thank God," Rob said.

"We got to her just in time but she lost a lot of blood and we need to keep an eye on her. I'll let you know when we move her to a new room."

"Thank you, doctor." He assumed that's what she was. "Thank you so much." The woman smiled and went back behind the door. Rob sat down and closed his eyes to breathe a sigh of relief. He heard the click of shoe heels against the hall floor. They moved fast and Rob craned his neck to see past the wall. It was Detective Hillman.

"You've got to be kidding me," he said to himself.

"Mr. Marshall," Hillman said as he got closer. "Imagine my surprise. There I was just about to head home when over the radio I hear an emergency call to your address."

"And you came all the way down here to check how we're doing," Rob said. "How thoughtful. How's your jaw?"

Hillman smirked and touched his face but carried on.

"Girl at the desk said Gina's gonna pull through. Lucky." Rob just nodded his head, skeptical of Hillman's tone. "Boy, trouble just seems to find you. Doesn't it, Rob?"

"Get the hell out of here, Hillman," Rob said.

"Sure thing." Hillman pulled out his black notepad and leaned against the wall. "Right after I get your statement." He clicked his pen and the sound brought Rob back to the night they met. Hillman's smug satisfaction was written all over his round face. There was no doubt that he relished the moment. Before he could start, the doctor came back out to collect Rob.

"Mr. Marshall," she said. "Follow me."

"Is she awake?" Rob said.

"She'll be in and out for the next little while, but yes, she's awake." Rob followed the doctor through the big doorway and Hillman clicked his pen closed.

"I'll be in touch, Rob."

"Can't wait," Rob said without looking back.

He walked behind the doctor through an endless maze of hallways until she stopped in front of a small room. Rob peered in and saw Gina. She was asleep, surrounded by tubes and machines. Rob sat in the chair next to the bed and listened to the soft rhythmic beeps of the equipment. He had the melody of the tones memorized within a few minutes. Gina flopped her head now and then but stayed asleep for a while. Rob leaned his head back on the chair and closed his eyes for a minute.

"Rob?" Gina said. Her throat sounded dry and cracked. Rob sat up and leaned close to her. Her eyes were barely open.

"Gina, I'm here," Rob whispered and touched her cheek.

"Where's Alex?" she said.

"What?"

"Make sure he does his homework," she said and closed her eyes again. She must have been dreaming. Rob leaned back in his chair and rested, too.

He was woken when a nurse bashed her clipboard against something metal.

"Sorry," she said quietly and left. There was a folder on the side table and Rob picked it up. There were some pamphlets and papers with the names of psychiatrists in the area. The early morning sun peeked in through the curtains and Rob decided to find the cafeteria. He wandered around the hallways until he found a map on a wall and got going in the right direction. He bought two coffees and headed to Gina's room. When he got back, a doctor was coming out with the nurse and they stepped aside to let him in.

"She's awake now," the nurse said. Rob was happy that he could talk to her.

"Gina?" he said as he walked in. She was sitting upright and wiping tears from her eyes.

"Oh, Rob," she said and sniffled. "I feel so stupid."

"Is everything OK?"

"Of course it's not. Look at me."

"Honey, we're gonna get through this," Rob said as he set the coffees down. He pointed at the folder on the table. "We'll get you the best help there is."

"And what about us?" she said as she looked up at him.

"What about us?"

"I miss you, Rob." Tears rolled down her cheeks and Rob grabbed a tissue as he sat down in the chair. He dabbed her face gently.

"I'm right here, Gina," he said. "I'm not going anywhere." Gina perked up and looked at the coffee cups.

"Is that for me?" she said. Rob looked over his shoulder and nodded. "Smells good." Rob passed one to her and his hand brushed against the bandage on her wrist. She recoiled when she felt his touch and they enjoyed their coffee in silence.

They kept Gina another night before they let her go. A home nurse stopped by every morning to change her bandages until Rob felt comfortable enough to do it himself. He took time off work to take care of Gina, much to his bosses delight. Rob took care of the shopping and cooking. He kept the house clean and tidy. They spent their days together instead of living separate lives that only intersected a couple of times a day. Rob was surprised that he hadn't found himself in Hillman's warpath but was happy not to have seen him.

Gina started seeing a therapist a few times a week like the hospital staff suggested. Rob didn't bug her for details. He just made sure things were easy for her at home. On the days she went to therapy, Rob would go to work. He scaled back on his duties so he wouldn't be overloaded. After a couple months, Gina suggested they see a couples counselor. Her therapist even recommended one for them. Rob wouldn't have agreed, but he remembered what Gina said in the hospital bed. *I miss you, Rob.* He told her he would go only if it didn't conflict with her own sessions. She set it up and once a week they had an appointment with Dr. Touré.

On the day of their first session, Rob waited at the door for her to get ready. Gina came around the corner wearing a short sleeved shirt for the first time since she was in the hospital.

"What do you think, honey?" she said as she struck a pose with her arms stretched out.

"Ah, you do have arms," Rob said.

"You can't even notice, can you?" she said and held her wrists in front of herself.

"You look great, hon," Rob said. "C'mon, we're gonna be late."

They drove to the office building. It wasn't very far. Just over on Lee Street. Rob checked the directory and the office was on the top floor. They rode the elevator up and Gina smiled without showing her teeth as she bobbed her head to the music. They checked in the with the receptionist and Rob looked out the window. He could see the river and some yachts docked at a marina. The woman at the desk called them in a few minutes later. She led them through the office hall to a large room. Its dark wood panels and brown furniture was a stark contrast to the bright and clinical waiting room. It was nicer than most living rooms. On either side of the big leather couch was a side table topped with a box of tissues. The barren coffee table separated the couch from a matching chair with a high back and tall arm rests. There was a desk at the back of the room that was as big as the couch, but it was dwarfed by the massive bookshelf behind it. Rob whistled as he looked around and Gina sat down on the couch. She patted the cushion beside her and Rob joined her.

He tapped his fingers on Gina's knee while they waited for the doctor to come in.

"Don't be nervous, Rob."

"I'm not," he said. "I'm just—" Before he could finish, a woman opened the door.

"Hi, guys. I'm Dr. Rashida Touré." She held a large notebook under her arm and held her hand out across the coffee table.

"I'm Rob. This is Gina. Nice to meet you." They shook hands and Dr. Touré sat in her chair across from them.

"Well let's get right to it, shall we?" she said. Gina nodded and smiled. "What brings you guys in to see me?"

"Where to begin?" Gina said.

"Just start at the beginning."

"Well, I suppose everything changed six months ago when our son, Alex, was kidnapped."

"Oh," Touré said as she shifted in her chair. Rob sensed her realization that this wasn't going to be the usual case of nitpicking spouses. She put her pen to the paper and scribbled down some notes. "Did you get him back?"

"No," Gina said. "Not yet."

"That will certainly put a lot of strain on a relationship." Touré regained her professional composure and relaxed in her seat. "Let's start there. Tell me everything."

Rob and Gina spent the session sharing the whole experience, taking turns when the memories proved too painful to continue. Touré nodded and wrote on her notepad as they spoke. Her watch beeped, but she insisted they keep going past the allotted hour.

"Basically, the case went cold and we had to try and move on," Rob said. Touré put her notes down on her lap while Gina dabbed her eyes with a tissue.

"I think that's enough for today," Touré said as she checked her watch. "We'll pick up from here next time."

"Thank you, Doctor," Gina said as they all stood up. Touré smiled and walked them to the door. Rob paid the receptionist with a check.

"Same time next week?" she said.

"You bet." Rob looked at the receipt as he turned around. It seemed like a lot of money for them to do all the talking. They'd done the exact same thing at their support group for free. He hoped next time they would get some actual advice.

Rob opened the car door for Gina and got in on his side. As they drove, Gina smiled contentedly but then jolted in her chair as if struck by a memory.

"Oh, I almost forgot," she said.

"What's that, hon?"

"That detective, what was his name? Oh right, Detective Hillman."

"What about him?" Rob said as he glanced between Gina and the road.

"He stopped by to check on us while you were out the other day. Isn't that nice of him?"

"Yeah." Rob chuckled in disbelief. "He's one of a kind."

"Anyway, he wanted me to tell you he hasn't forgotten about the case."

"I don't expect he would," Rob said. Gina settled in her seat and smiled as she looked back out the window.

I don't expect he would, Rob thought.

- 10 -

Rob and Gina went about their week as usual. Dr. Touré got them to do some exercises that were designed to promote good communication. Every week she had some more tips and tricks to help them, but Rob felt it was all just too generalized.

They sat on the big, comfortable couch and Touré came in right on time as always.

"Alright, guys. Let's get going," she said. Rob sensed a difference in her manner that day. She had always been the listener. An astute moderator to facilitate as they spoke but, on that day, she seemed poised to take charge. "I feel like we've got a good base here and it's time we dig deeper to help move forward," she said. Rob couldn't have agreed more. Up until then, he felt they could have plucked the same advice from the pages of one of the women's magazines in the waiting room.

"Absolutely," he said.

"I want you to go back to the day your son disappeared. But this time I want feelings, not facts. OK?" They both nodded their heads and Gina started.

"It all happened so fast. The school called and I panicked. I called Rob on my way there. I remember running around the school to check all the rooms and I think scared some of the teachers and kids, but I didn't care. I almost couldn't breathe, but I kept going. Mrs. Weaver, she was the principal, couldn't keep up with me. Her stupid high heels clicked behind me and it made me mad. She just seemed more concerned with updating everyone instead of helping me look. We just finished searching inside the school and then Rob got there."

"And what about you, Rob?" Touré said as she turned in her chair to face him. He recounted his frantic drive to the school and the conversation in Mrs. Weaver's office. The pain of that day came back full force as he spoke. Gina interrupted him.

"I always knew that school was bad news. We should have sent him to Ryerson Academy."

"This again?" Rob said. "You know, we both made the decision to put him in public school."

"Yeah. You thought it was too much money," Gina said. "Just look at what that choice cost us." She looked away from Rob and rested her chin on her hand. His blood boiled inside his veins as he took a deep breath. The trouble was, he couldn't help but think that she was right. Ever since the day Alex disappeared, that thought had weighed on him. Gina was right; it was only money, and he would give every last bit of it away if it meant that he could see his little boy again. His guilt gave way to anger at Gina's callous finger pointing.

"You're right, Gina," Rob said. "This is all my fault. I should have known that some psychopath would kidnap our son if we cheaped out and sent him to public school. How stupid of me." Touré leaned back in her chair and intervened before things went too far.

"We're not here to place blame. That won't do either of you any good. Gina, tell me what happened next."

Gina shifted her gaze after a quick glance in Rob's direction and continued on about the police and the FBI. Rob had his turn but left out the incident with Detective Hillman. He didn't want to give Gina another reason to look down her nose at him.

When their session ended, they both got up quicker than usual, happy to be done reliving the horrible ordeal. They drove home in silence and, once they arrived, resumed their separate habits. Rob on the couch and Gina in the office. Talking things over with a therapist was meant to help them be a better couple but so far it had only driven a wedge between them.

Rob had the afternoon off that day and went for a drive. He was still mad at Gina for her private school remark and needed to get out of the house for a bit. He drove along the parkway that overlooked the river and found himself in Arlington. He didn't go there much and he was just about to turn around and head back to Alexandria when a shooting range caught his eye. He never had any interest in guns before but figured it would be a nice distraction from everything going on. Plus, he'd never fired a gun before. Some guys from work invited him along once, but he declined. They talked about it for weeks afterward and he decided to see what all the fuss was about.

The short man at the front desk took all of Rob's information. He even took a thumbprint on the consent form. The short man rhymed off all of the safety rules and showed Rob some guns. His voice was louder than necessary, like someone who just walked out of a loud concert. He recommended a little silver .22 pistol since it was best for first-timers. Rob nodded along with a feigned understanding, but he didn't know the first thing about what the man said. He followed the man to the back and they both got some earplugs and big earmuffs. The pops and bangs of the other shooters were stifled until the man opened another door. It wasn't loud, but Rob could still hear every shot. The man led him to an empty station and placed the gun on the black counter. He showed Rob the right way to hold the gun. It was mostly visual instruction because of the noise, but the man shouted anyway. He pointed two fingers at his eyes to signal Rob to watch closely. The man took aim, slid his index finger down from the barrel, and squeezed the trigger. Rob nodded at him and the man put the pistol down on the counter again. He stepped back and motioned for Rob to come and take his place.

He approached with extreme caution as if somehow the gun would go off on its own if he didn't sneak up on it. The man slapped Rob on the shoulder to encourage him and took him by the wrist. He guided his hand to pick up the silver gun. Rob naturally put his finger inside the trigger guard, but the man wagged his finger at him and Rob remembered the safe way to hold it. They pointed it toward the target and the man stepped back. Rob's arms were locked in place, but he looked over for instruction. The man held his hands up like he had an imaginary gun and exaggerated a trigger pull, but he shook his head to say that was wrong. He moved his index finger back and forth and nodded up and down before he gave Rob a thumbs up to fire his first shot.

Rob focused his aim at the target and squeezed the trigger. The gun kicked back against his grip and he felt the force of it through his arms and shoulders. He even felt it in his neck. Even with the ear protection, it was loud and he was exhilarated. He smiled and the man motioned toward the target for Rob to shoot again. He kept at it until he used up all the ammunition he paid for. The man gave him the paper target as a keepsake. Rob missed a few times, but most of his shots hit the mark. He put it in the trunk of his car and headed home; a smile on his face the whole way.

"Where'd you get off to?" Gina said as he walked in.

"Went to a shooting range."

"Fine, don't tell me," Gina said and shuffled back to the office. Rob shook his head at her implication. After everything, she still didn't trust him. He went back to the car to get his target and left it on the kitchen table.

Rob had the television on when she finally emerged to make dinner and she spotted his souvenir. She turned around and smiled at him. She came over and sat down next to him with her legs curled up so she leaned against him. They looked each other in the eyes Gina gave him a long kiss. When she pulled away, a spark of curiosity filled her face.

"What was it like?" she said.

"Loud, terrifying, and a little painful," Rob said and laughed through his nose. "It was amazing."

- 11 -

Their next session with Dr. Touré was canceled and Gina suggested they do something together. All week Rob had seen her stop and look at his hole-riddled target which, for some reason, was still on the kitchen table. He asked her to go for a drive with him and see where the road took them. She agreed and he drove toward Arlington. When he pulled up to the shooting range, Gina's eyes lit up with surprise. She bounced across the parking lot and Rob held the door open for her. The faint pops of shots being fired widened her eyes and she smiled at him. The short man was there to greet them and he recognized Rob.

"Figured you'd be back," he said. "Want the Mark-III again?" Rob nodded.

After they were done, Gina couldn't stop talking about it the whole way home. Rob was elated that they had found something to do together. He hadn't seen Gina that happy in a long time. Her smile stretched across her face as she admired her target.

"We should make this a regular thing," Gina said as Rob held the front door for her.

"I'd like that very much," he said.

They spent more time together that week. Dinners out, movie nights, and anything else they could think of. It was just like they were newlyweds again. They arrived at their next therapy session with an exuberance that seemed to please Dr. Touré.

"Alright," Touré said with a knowing smile, "what happened?"

"What do you mean?" Rob said.

"Come on, spill it, you two." Touré was almost laughing. "You guys were practically at each other's throats last time and now you look like a couple of high school sweethearts." Rob and Gina smiled at each other. "You've obviously turned a corner. I want to know all about it."

Rob and Gina told her all about the shooting range like excited children recounting their summer vacation on the first day of school. They told her about their week and all the romantic things they did together. Touré smiled and nodded along as they spoke, clearly impressed with their renewed affection for each other. She exhaled as she laid down her notepad and pen on her legs.

"This is great progress," she said. "We still have work to do, but it's a big step forward."

They finished up a few minutes later and on the ride home, Gina leaned herself toward Rob. She batted her eyelashes so hard they could have caused a breeze. He could always tell when she wanted something.

"Yes?" Rob said.

"Let's go away somewhere," she said.

"What? Where?"

"I don't know," she said with a shrug and sat back in her seat. "Just away."

"A balloon ride around the world, then?"

"Don't be silly, Rob. Oh! How about the caverns in Shenandoah? We always wanted to see those but never made it out there."

"You're serious?"

"Why not?"

Rob pondered his weekend plans of television and housework and came to the same conclusion.

"You're right, Gina. Why not?"

"Really?" Gina smiled wide.

"Yeah. Let's do it."

"Oh, Rob, it'll be great. We can take the

Skyline Drive, see the mountains, maybe get a cozy hotel room. Make a weekend out of it."

"That sounds wonderful," Rob said. He thought he glimpsed a familiar car in his mirror, but the glare of the sun blocked his view. He dismissed it and turned the corner of their street. When they got home, Gina took a straight shot to the computer so she could check out some hotels online. When she resurfaced, she rubbed her eyes as she came down the hall.

"Any luck?" Rob said. Gina waved him over and he followed. She showed him a bunch of places in they could stay in Shenandoah and they picked a charming colonial bed and breakfast that was just a quick drive from the caverns. Rob left to start on dinner and Gina called the hotel to make reservations.

"Good news, Rob," she called out. "The big room is ours this weekend."

"Can't wait," he said.

Gina went out to do some shopping for the trip after they ate. Rob watched the Red Sox game and dozed off on the couch. He was awoken by the sound of keys jingling outside the door. He may have been groggy, but he thought he heard Gina talking to someone. He stretched and opened the door in time to see Detective Hillman's car drive away.

"Gina," he said as he rubbed his eyes, "was

that—"

"Did you fall asleep watching the game again?" Gina smiled as she ran a finger down an indent in his face, left there by the fabric of the sofa. "Honestly, Rob, I don't know why you watch baseball if it's so boring."

"It's not boring, it's relaxing," Rob said and rubbed his cheek. "Who were you just talking to?"

"Huh? Oh, Detective Hillman stopped by to check in on us. He didn't have anything new to report. Told him about our trip." Gina sighed as she put her bags down on the table. "Won't it be nice to get away from it all, Rob?"

Rob was immediately suspicious of Hillman but got distracted by the pink bag that stood out amongst the others. He knew which store it was from.

"Have fun shopping?" He smiled eagerly and pointed his eyes toward the table. Gina snatched it up and held it close.

"That's a surprise and you can't see it yet!" She laughed as she turned her body away from him. Rob held his arms out and shuffled toward her. His hands found their way to her hips and he kissed her neck.

"Just a sneak preview?"

Gina pulled away from him.

"Close the door," she said as she walked

backward toward their room. "What would the neighbors think?" He closed it as fast as he could and followed her to the bedroom.

- 12 -

The day had finally come and Rob packed his things last minute.

"What's the weather gonna be like again?" he called out to Gina.

"Seasonal," she said from the bathroom.

"What does that even mean?" he said to himself but Gina must have heard him.

"It means bring a jacket."

"Thank you!" he called back in recognition of Gina's superhuman hearing.

Rob loaded their suitcases in the back of the car while Gina set the timer for the lights and armed the security system. As he closed the trunk, he squinted at the car parked way down the street.

"You're sure you've got everything?" Gina said from the porch. Rob shook his head and turned around. He patted his pockets to check.

"Yep, yep, and yep," he said as his hands slapped against his pants. "Good to go."

Gina shut the door and skipped down the steps toward the car. He held the car door open for her and watched her smile wide as he walked around to his side.

"Ready?" she said.

"Let's blow this popsicle stand," Rob said as he started the engine. They laughed and he drove off. The beige car down the street stayed where it was and Rob put it out of his mind.

"Better fill up before we hit the interstate," Rob said. He stopped at a station not far from their house and, as he pumped the gas, he saw a beige car stop in a parking lot across the street. He tried to dismiss it as paranoia though he couldn't help but try to spy the driver. He finished at the pump and went in to pay. He took his time inside and tried to look casual as he browsed the aisles, his eyes never on the goods but fixed on the beige car. It taunted him. The longer Rob took in the store, the more his suspicion grew. It had to be Hillman. Rob grabbed some drinks and a map and headed to the counter. He paid without a glance toward the attendant and left. Gina noticed his obsessive stare when he got back in the car.

"What are you looking at, Rob?" He snapped out of it.

"Nothing," he said and handed her the map. "Here. You are now the world's sexiest navigator."

"Well aren't you lucky?" Gina said. Rob drove off and kept an eye on his mirror. The beige car stayed where it was so he relaxed and enjoyed the ride. Once they hit the interstate, the hustle of the city died down more and more until just the sound of the wind ripped past the open car windows. Gina breathed in the fresh summer air and Rob patted her thigh as they shared a smile. She grabbed the maps and unfolded it. It rippled against the wind, almost tearing from the force and Rob rolled the windows up to help her. The tranquil drive was interrupted from time to time by the toll booths scattered along the highway.

"After this one, we need to take sixty-six west," Gina said.

"Aye, aye, navigator," Rob said and saluted. Gina giggled at his antics. They held hands as Rob drove. With the morning sun behind them, Rob looked ahead to the open road, happy to leave it all behind. No housework, no therapists, no meetings or mindless office functions. Just a man and his wife, headed to the middle of nowhere to be alone with each other.

Rob put on the rock station and they sang along with some of their favorite tunes. Every time Rob looked over at Gina, she seemed completely happy and he couldn't help but feel the same. As the sun rose higher, it peeked its way through the billows of clouds in sharp, defined beams of light. The sections of tree-lined highway opened up to reveal vast expanses of farmland and rolling fields. They cruised by the small towns that beckoned travelers with outlet malls and eateries. Gina looked at her map and ran a searching finger along their route.

"We should stop at this little diner for some lunch before we get on Skyline Drive."

"Do you really want to take Skyline?"

"Yeah, it sounds great."

"But you can only go like thirty-five," Rob said. "It would be faster if we just go around the park and straight to the caverns."

"You in a rush?" Gina said.

"Well, no. It's just..." Rob trailed off and gave in with a shake of his head. Gina switched looks between the map and the signs on the side of the road.

"Take the next exit," she said.

Rob pulled up to the restaurant and they got out. Rob stretched his legs against the tires before they went in. A young waitress handed them some menus and showed them to a table. By the time they sat down, two men were standing by Rob's car. Ever suspicious, he kept an eye on them through the window but they just pointed at the vehicle and nodded to each other.

They ordered their lunch and Gina rambled off a bunch of tidbits about the park. The curious men at Rob's car wandered off just as the waitress brought the food over. While they ate, the glint of the sun bounced off of the windshield of a beige car at the far end of the lot. The glare blocked Rob's view of the driver.

"Doesn't that sound great, Rob?" Gina said as she touched his hand. He hadn't heard a word she said.

"You bet."

"What are you looking at?"

"That beige car over there," Rob said. "Isn't that Detective Hillman's car?"

"What would he be doing all the way out here? Following us?" Gina laughed her question off. "Rob, there's a million beige cars in the world."

"You're probably right."

"Come on, let's hit the road, Mr. Paranoid," she said.

They drove off and in a few minutes they

had finally reached Skyline Drive. The road wasn't very busy and it offered spectacular views after every twist and turn. Rob caught himself going faster than the posted limit a few times and had to correct his speed. Gina made a gleeful comment for every wildlife sighting along the way. Rob kept a watchful eye in his rear view but shook his head at the absurd idea. There was no way the detective would follow them all the way out here. It was extreme, even for Hillman. Rob decided to let it go and give himself over to the adventure.

Mile after mile, the mountains overlapped in the distance until they were but shadows against the horizon. He couldn't help but think that Alex would have loved the view. Gina leaned forward in her seat to search the glove box and flopped back in defeat.

"Damn," she said.

"What is it?"

"The map," Gina said. "I think I left it in that diner." Rob chuckled.

"It's not funny, Rob."

"Look up ahead, honey," he said as he pointed his chin toward the big entrance station. "Thornton Gap. Isn't that where we need to get off?"

Gina breathed a sigh of relief and Rob got on the highway, headed West to the caverns.

Rob was sick of puttering along and accelerated hard once back on the highway. The car lunged and the engine clunked as the gears changed. Rob brushed it off as a bad shift and carried on. He weaved from lane to lane as he passed by the slower cars. He thought of Alex again and pressed his foot down on the gas pedal. He hadn't gotten angry about it in a long time but, at that moment, mere hours from his boy's birthday, he felt enraged that he wasn't there. Their house could have been filled with his little friends from school. A big party with cake and presents and fun instead of two grief-stricken parents trying their best not to mention it to each other on a trip that was nothing more than a thin distraction from their pain.

The wind roared in through the open windows and blew Gina's long hair back. She tensed in her seat and gripped the door handle.

"Um, Rob?"

He clenched his fingers tight around the steering wheel and sped on without an answer. His eyes fixed ahead as he spotted his openings in the traffic.

"Rob slow down!" Gina yelled. He ignored her plea as he pushed the pedal down even further on a straightaway.

"Are you trying to kill us?" Gina shouted over the sound of the wind. She pressed the buttons to roll up the windows and the car sputtered and clunked as it slowed down.

"Oh that's just great, Rob," Gina said as she threw her hands up. "What the hell is wrong with you?" He shook his head and pulled the car off to a side road as it lost momentum and finally stopped in the gravel of the shoulder.

"I'll try restarting it," Rob said.

"Oh please. You broke the car, you maniac. I can't believe you."

"It's going to be fine," he said as he released the key and slid it back in. The engine clicked as he turned it and refused the start. He unbuckled his belt and popped the hood. Gina followed him out and continued to scold him.

"And what do you think you're going to do?" she said as he leaned against the open hood.

"Something probably just came loose," he said as he surveyed the perplexing array of hoses and metal parts. He could barely identify any of the components let alone repair them. He circled the car and kicked the tires. He crouched to see underneath, but there was no apparent sign of what the problem was. He arched back to stretch as he stood and looked down the long side road in search of some sign of civilization. The afternoon sun had turned a soft orange as it started to set and cast long shadows as Rob looked back to the highway. As the transport trucks drove past, he spotted another car on the shoulder nearly out of view.

"Well, I'll just call a tow truck," he said as he pulled out his cell phone. "No service. Piece of shit phone." He peered off in the distance as Gina tapped her toes on the gravel, her arms crossed in anger.

"What now, Mr. Daredevil?" Gina said. He figured their best chance was that the road led to a town and a garage.

"This road has to lead somewhere," he said as he pointed toward nothing. "And don't act like this is my fault. I didn't plan for the car to break down, you know."

"If you weren't driving like a lunatic then we wouldn't be stuck in the middle of nowhere. Now we'll never get to the caverns."

"You're the one who just *had* to take Skyline. Big deal. A bunch of trees and deer. Good call, Gina."

"You can be a real asshole sometimes, Rob."

"Name calling. That's very helpful right now," he said. "Let's just get walking. Maybe someone will let us use their phone."

Gina huffed in disgust and Rob locked the car as they walked away.

- 13 -

Dust kicked up like little clouds behind their feet as they shuffled along the side of the road. The pavement had long given way to gravel and dirt. The house in the distance never seemed to get any closer no matter how many steps they took. They spoke no words and kept a distance between each other. Gina was still incensed and walked with her arms crossed, an indication of blame. Rob surveyed the land as he trod, occasionally checking for a signal on his phone. He spied Gina's backward glance every so often as he squinted in the setting sun. It barely peeked over the horizon and would give way to dusk at any moment. With every bend in the road, the silhouette of the house appeared closer. It wouldn't be long until they arrived. Rob kicked a rock from his path and hoped that someone was there. It could have been abandoned for all he knew.

At last, the final rays of sunlight shone across the fields and the blinding sun dipped out of sight, leaving nothing but a soft glow in the sky as the blue darkness crept up behind them. No cars came upon them. No good samaritans to rescue them from their arduous trek.

The dirt path curved around some large trees and opened to a clear view of the house. It was close but still a good walk away. Night had fallen and a light flicked on. The shape of a person moved past the window and another room lit up. Rob was relieved that at least someone was home and his slow march became a hopeful stroll. He caught up to Gina and matched her pace. She ambled on, eyes fixed on the house. Her posture had relaxed, too. They walked side by side until they reached the driveway. They both stopped at the entrance and stared down the long, rutted lane that led to the house. Gina took Rob's hand and they set off past the nondescript mailbox that stood just outside a makeshift entry gate of old fence wood propped up in a triangle on either side. They each walked in one of the grooves left by repeated trips up and down the unpaved drive. As they neared, the soft glow of a light upstairs cut to black and a few seconds later a yellow bulb flickered to life on the front porch. Now just steps away, they heard the door squeak and click before it opened.

A tall woman stood behind the screen door and her head moved from side to side as she tried to make out the incoming strangers.

"Who's there?" she called out.

"Hello, ma'am," Rob said and held up a hand as they stopped their approach. "Our car died just off the highway and we've got no signal. We were wondering, that is, if it's not—"

"Please, can we use your phone?" Gina cut in. The woman's chin pushed out as she peered at them through the screen. The door creaked as she opened it and stepped outside.

"You poor things," the woman said. Her frizzy hair blew around in the wind and she wrung her hands together as she looked back down the dirt road. "Of course. Come in, come in."

"Oh thank you," Gina said with a sigh.

"Don't you mention it. Name's Darlene, by the way." She came down the noisy wood steps and held out her hand. They shook and introduced themselves. Darlene led them to the porch but stopped in front of the door. "All's I ask is we keep our voices down. Just put the little one to bed, you see."

Rob smiled and put a finger against his lips as he nodded. Darlene held the door and waved them inside. "Sorry if I seemed rude. We just don't get too many visitors."

They stepped in and Darlene shut the doors behind her. Rob looked around the front hall. It was dark in the spots where the dim lights didn't reach. The wall of the staircase leading up was littered with old looking sepia or black and white photographs of people from another era. There were framed cross-stitch quotations like Bless This House and Home Is Where The Heart Is. Everything looked antique and time-tested. Even the wood railing of the stairs was smooth from many years of use. An ancient grandfather clock in the hallway ticked away as its pendulum swung. Darlene pointed at a small round table with a yellow rotary phone on it.

"Well, there it is," she said.

"Thank you so much." Rob was overly quiet. Gina raised her nose in the air.

"It smells wonderful in here. I hope we aren't interrupting your dinner."

"No, no," Darlene said. "My husband, Marvin, is on his way home. I like to have supper ready when he gets in."

Rob listened to them make small talk while he waited on hold for the tow company. He couldn't use the automated system with the relic telephone so he had to wait and wait. He heard Darlene offer them coffee, but he shook his head and mouthed a polite decline. The two women went back to the kitchen and, when Rob finished with his phone call, he joined them.

"Bad news, hon," Rob said as he looked at his watch. "Looks like it'll be about three hours before they can get a truck out."

Gina looked at him, devastated.

"You're joking."

"Well, at least we have plenty of time to hoof it back to the car," Rob said. Darlene watched with a wide-eyed wonder as they spoke and raised her hand to interject. They both looked over at her.

"There'll be none of that," she said. "It's much too far to walk all the way back to the highway. My Marvin will be home any minute and he can drive you back."

"But you're about to have dinner and you've already been too kind," Gina said.

"Nonsense," Darlene said as she stirred a big pot on the stove. "You're welcome to join us. You must be starving after that long hike."

"We wouldn't want to impose," Rob said.

"I insist. Now just sit right down and rest those feet." Rob felt it would be rude to refuse her after she helped them so he conceded and sat down. Gina expressed an unwillingness but Rob shrugged his shoulders at her and smirked. It wouldn't hurt them to be sociable for an hour or two. He didn't exactly relish the thought of the long trudge back to the car either. Besides, Darlene had a welcoming way about her. Rob hoped her husband wouldn't mind that two complete strangers were in his house, though. People live way out in the middle of nowhere for a reason; to be left alone.

Darlene lifted the lid from the big pot again and steam billowed out as she stirred. She licked the spoon to taste it and smacked her lips in approval. Just then, headlights cast moving shadows across the walls. Rob and Gina looked out the window from the table and Darlene kept at her preparation.

"That'll be Marvin now," she said. "Perfect timing."

- 14 -

After so many months without incident, Marvin's nerves began to calm. Nobody had come around to the house. Nobody asked any questions. The last time the DC papers mentioned Alex was when the principal of his school was transferred God knows where as a punishment. The teacher was let go, too. He figured it was all to avoid a lawsuit. People loved to sue each other in the city. Once the finger pointing started, Marvin assumed the Feds had given up and moved on to the next case.

That summer was a perfect mix of rain and sun. It afforded him a lot of time to spend with Mikey and Darlene. They increased their farm work. He hoped, sooner rather than later, they could all work the land and be full-time farmers. Darlene taught Mikey math and writing in the afternoons while Marvin made his deliveries. They would take trips into the mountains on the weekends, never too far from home, and teach him about nature as they hiked through the wilderness.

One summer evening, Marvin headed back home after a late delivery. The setting sun had turned a blood red in the distance. He pulled off the highway and slowed down when he saw two cars on the side of the road. A man with a flashlight peered inside one car. Marvin slowed to a stop beside him and rolled his window down.

"Having some car trouble?"

The man looked at Marvin, his round face suspicious as he stepped over to the truck.

"You recognize this car, sir?" He shone the light in Marvin's face.

"Nope. Need a hand?"

The man stroked his mustache as he pointed his light around inside the truck. He had the manner of a cop, but he wasn't a county sheriff. Marvin's heart skipped a beat and his eyes fixed on the glove box as the flashlight searched around.

"No thanks," he said. "Move along, sir."

Marvin drove off slowly along the rough road. Old nerves came back but the further along the road he got, the more he settled. The soft lights from the windows of the house in the distance soothed him and soon he was home. He stopped at the mailbox, but it was empty, as usual. When he pulled up, Darlene was waiting for him on the porch. She came down the steps to meet him and he tucked the gun from the glove box in the back of his pants before she got there.

- 15 -

Gina looked around the small dining area.

"My God, Rob. Can you believe this place?"

"What do you mean?"

"Rotary phone. Grandfather clock. Dirt path driveway. Rickety everything. Even her clothes. Did we go back in time or something?" Gina laughed in disbelief.

"Be nice," he said. "We'd be hitchhiking if it wasn't for these people. It's just for a little bit. You know, it doesn't look much different than that fancy bed and breakfast you booked for us. If you saw this place online you'd be all over it." They both laughed and Gina reached across to hold his hand.

"Rob, listen," she said as she stared in his eyes. "About earlier—"

Rob knew she was about to apologize but

the squeaky door announced the return of their hosts and they both stood up. Marvin stepped in and kicked his loose boots onto a rubber mat. He was a mountain of a man, a full head taller than Rob and twice as wide. His shoulders drove out from his neck when he turned to face them. His head cocked to the side as he looked at them as if he had seen them before but just couldn't place it. His eyes darted between them and the staircase. Rob could tell he was uncomfortable with visitors.

"Heard y'all had some trouble on the road," he said and held his massive hand out to Rob. "Name's Marvin."

"I'm Rob. This is my wife, Gina." Marvin's hand swallowed up Rob's and his grip was like a torturous vise for the few seconds they shook. Marvin kept glancing up the stairs as they greeted each other. Gina had to crane her neck to look up at him and waved.

"We're so sorry to intrude like this."

"Think nothing of it," Marvin said. His voice boomed even at a low volume. "Whaddya say we have a nice quick supper and then I'll take ya to meet that tow truck?"

"Sounds great," Gina said. "And thank you again. You're very kind."

Darlene set the table and served a piping hot soup. Rob was starved and picked up his spoon. He was about to scoop up a mouthful when he heard Marvin clear his throat. He had joined hands with Gina and Darlene and they all looked at Rob. He put his spoon down and Marvin closed his eyes before he spoke.

"Dear Lord, thank you for this wonderful bounty. May you watch over us in our travels. Amen."

"That was lovely, Marvin. Thank you," Gina said.

"Welp, sounds like you could use all the help you can get right now," Marvin said and chuckled. His gaze never left Rob and Gina, even as he ate. It was rather discomforting, but Rob put himself in Marvin's shoes. A couple of strangers he didn't know from a hole in the ground would make Rob uneasy, too. He wouldn't even have opened the door if it were him, let alone serve them dinner.

"Mikey go to sleep okay?" Marvin asked his wife. She nodded. Their spoons chimed against the ceramic bowls as they ate. Marvin nodded along with her. "Well, that's good."

"How old is he?" Gina said.

"He'll be seven tomorrow," Darlene said and smiled wide.

"Tomorrow?"

"That's right."

Gina let her spoon rest in the bowl and drew in a sharp breath. Rob sensed her dismay and placed his hand on top of hers.

"Everything alright?" Darlene said, her eyebrows raised high on her forehead. Marvin had stopped eating and looked at them with concern.

"Forgive me," Gina said. Rob tapped her hand and explained.

"It's our son's birthday tomorrow, too."

"What a coincidence!" Darlene said. "How old?"

"He's, um, not with us anymore," Rob said. Darlene looked confused and opened her mouth as if she was about to ask another question when Marvin stopped her.

"Sorry to hear that, Rob. Darlene, these people have had a rough go of it today. They don't need to be interrogated."

Darlene went back to her soup and Marvin slit his eyes as he looked at Rob. Thankfully, Marvin changed the subject. "Pretty sure I know you from somewhere." He pointed his spoon at Rob.

"I get that a lot. I've just got one of those faces."

"Naw, naw. It's bugging me to no end. Where'd ya go to school?"

"University of Chicago."

"Oh." Marvin sounded defeated. Rob

figured his host wasn't an Ivy League alumni. "How about high school? In Chicago too, I guess." Rob nodded. "That wouldn't be it then. Oh well. Y'all on your way to New York or something?"

"No," Rob said. "We live in Alexandria now. Just outside DC. We came out to the country to get away for the weekend."

Marvin leaned in closer as Rob spoke. His brow furrowed down. Rob felt like Marvin was trying his best to figure him out. He tried to focus on his meal. Gina had composed herself and silently thanked Rob with a pat of her hand on his thigh.

"This soup is delicious, Darlene," Gina said.

"Why thank you." Her eyes lit up with pride. "Everything from our own garden, too. Even little Mikey helps me grow everything." She looked at Gina's arms and leaned her head forward for closer inspection. "Marvin, look," she said and held her forearm up. She traced her finger along a jagged line of white skin on the inside of her wrist. "We got the same scars!"

Marvin put his spoon in his bowl and huffed.

"Christ, Darlene," he said. "You don't say things like that."

"It's okay, Marvin," Gina said. Marvin shook his head in disapproval at his wife.

Darlene lowered her head.

"Sorry, Gina. I just never seen anyone else with them. Not outside the hospital anyway."

"Don't worry about it." Gina lowered a hand below the table and kept eating. Darlene seemed oblivious to the sensitivity of the subject and kept on.

"Mine are from a long while back," she said. "See, we'd been trying for a baby for quite some time. So many tests and gizmos and then we even tried that in veto thing."

"In vitro?" Gina said.

"That's the one. So we tried that and it was just so darn expensive but all I ever wanted was to be a mommy, you know?" Gina smiled at Darlene as she continued. "Time after time after time and we were at the point where we just couldn't afford another shot. I knew it was out last chance and, as always, it didn't work."

"Alright, Darlene. These folks don't need our life story." Marvin seemed disturbed by his wife's frankness, but she kept going.

"Well I was just heartbroken and I wasn't thinking straight. So here we are."

Rob pushed the story along for Gina's sake.

"But then you had Mikey so it all worked out in the end."

Darlene shook her head at Rob like he should have known that wasn't how it went.

"No, no. After all that, my Marvin surprised me one day." Marvin shifted with obvious discomfort.

"That's enough of about that," he said. He was firm and gruff, but Darlene ignored him. Like most parents, she seemed to relish the chance to boast about her child. Rob figured that living out in the middle of nowhere would have limited those opportunities.

"He brought Mikey home from an orphanage. He was so timid. He cried and cried. Must have gotten attached to the foster family. But I don't think they could have been treating him so good. Poor thing didn't even have a coat."

"Wait," Gina said. "Just like that? No interviews or screening or anything?"

"Nope. Marvin told me they was, uh, overburdened." She looked at her husband to confirm if she used the right word and Marvin nodded. He looked uncomfortable and kept his eye trained on Darlene.

"But—"

"So Rob, you a Nationals fan or White Sox?" Marvin cut Gina off.

"Ah, I'll watch whatever's on," Rob said. Gina laughed at him.

"You mean you'll fall asleep to whatever's on."

"It's relaxing," Rob said as he shrugged his

shoulders up. "Am I right, Marvin?"

"They don't understand."

The big man rose as everyone had finished their soup and Darlene helped him collect the dishes. Rob checked his watch and stood as well.

"Think I'll check in with the tow truck, if it's alright?"

"Be my guest," Marvin said. He helped Darlene with the washing up.

Gina followed Rob to the hallway and whispered to him as dialed on the old phone.

"Can you believe these rubes?" she said.

"Stop that. They're perfectly nice people."

"Who lets someone adopt a child after a suicide attempt? There's guns on the wall and everything."

"This isn't exactly the big city," Rob said. "Besides, they never really said Mikey was a person. Could be a dog for all we know."

They giggled and Rob held a finger to his lips to quiet her. He spoke to the dispatcher on the phone and nodded along.

"Yep. Uh-huh. Okay. Thanks." He hung up and scratched his forehead.

"What?" Gina pleaded for an update.

"She said it'll be another hour or so. Hopefully."

Gina tilted her head back and groaned.

"I just want to get out of here," she said.

"This place creeps me out."

Darlene poked her head around the corner.

"You guys want some coffee?" They agreed and sat back down at the table. Darlene brought a serving tray over and poured them each a cup. Rob stirred some cream with a tiny spoon that dinged against the glass. Marvin broke Rob's trance.

"Sorry, Rob, I just can't let it go," he said. "You sure we never met before?"

"Pretty sure. Happens to me all the time." Rob thought back to the press conference on their front lawn. "I've been on TV."

"Oh, my!" Darlene said. "A real-life celebrity in our house, Marvin." Rob laughed at the remark.

"Nothing like that. It was just a little thing on the news." He stirred his coffee again. Gina sniffled beside him and Rob noticed Marvin straighten up in his chair. His eyes widened and darted around the room. He almost dropped his mug but placed it on the tray. He breathed in loud, sharp bursts and his friendly manner was gone. He stood up fast, knocking the table with his knee. It shook the glasses and tapped his watch.

"You know," his voice shook the words out, "we really should head on back to your car."

"What's the hurry?" Darlene said.

"You just never know with those tow

trucks," Marvin said. "Don't want to miss it."

"At least let them finish their coffee, Marvin."

He nodded and sat back down, tapping his fingers. He glanced out the window every few minutes. Gina spoke with Darlene while Rob watched.

"Bet you guys have a big birthday party planned for tomorrow."

"Oh nothing much," Darlene said. "Just us three."

"Doesn't Mikey go to school around here?"

"Oh, no, I homeschool him. Marvin says it's for the best. Poor thing is so skittish all the time."

Gina looked at Rob with a complete lack of surprise and he shook his head at her antics. Sure they were a bit odd but he figured they were thinking the same thing about him and Gina.

"I'm making a big ole cake for him," Darlene said. "I want to make it special since it's his first birthday with us."

Rob cocked his head with curiosity.

"When did you adopt him?"

Marvin placed both his big hands on the table. His fingertips turned white as he pressed them down. He cleared his throat.

"I really think we should head out." Darlene carried on as if Marvin hadn't said a word.

"Happiest day of my life," she said. "November the third, last year."

Rob couldn't believe his ears. His stomach did a flip on itself and he felt the color drain from his face. It had to be a coincidence. Gina broke down next to him at the mention of the date. A million scenarios flashed through his mind. It couldn't be. The table creaked against Marvin's weight as he rose. Darlene casually got up and went on.

"Strangest thing, though. Marvin told me to pay it no never mind, but the poor boy insisted his name was Alex for the longest time."

- 16 -

As the words left Darlene's mouth, Marvin clamped his massive hand around Rob's arm and pulled him up out of his seat. Marvin's thick arm wrapped around his neck before he could react.

"Oh my God! Rob!" Gina yelled.

"Marvin what are you doing?" Darlene said, shocked. Marvin squeezed his forearm against Rob's throat and spoke through his teeth. His voice seethed with rage and panic.

"Why'd you have to come to this house? Why'd you have to keep asking?" Rob made a grunting noise but couldn't speak. His head filled with pressure. Marvin reached his free hand behind him and Gina screamed as he pulled a gun from the back of his belt. Gina rushed against the two of them and forced them against the brittle drywall. The gun fired a shot through the window and fell to the floor. Marvin heaved his free hand around and slapped Gina across the face. The force spun her and she fell to the floor. Rob tried to pull the huge arm away from his throat, but Marvin secured it with his other hand. He shouted as he pulled his grip tighter on Rob.

"So now you know! And I can't let you leave here!" He cinched tighter and tighter as he leaned back.

Rob's feet left the floor as he struggled against him. Little dots of light danced in his vision and the room darkened around him. Darlene stood in a state of shock, immobile. He saw Gina get to her hands and knees and shake her head as she crawled toward something in the hallway. Rob could feel the life being squeezed out of him and, in an almost euphoric state, he saw a shape on the stairway. The light cast across the face of a terrified boy. Alex. Was it real? He must have died. The blackness crept in around the house. This was it. Gina propped herself up on her knee and pointed the gun at him. Or was it at Marvin? His heartbeat thundered in his head as he kicked against the legs behind him. His senses heightened and failed in pulses. A sound of the front door as it crashed open. A familiar face came around the kitchen threshold. Silence, save for a thumping in his head. His final heartbeats, he assumed. Marvin jerked Rob's body.

"Let him go!" Detective Hillman shouted as he trained his weapon on Marvin. "Gina, drop the gun! Now!"

Rob felt the giant man give a hard squeeze. Gina looked at Rob, her face streaked with mascara.

"Don't do it, Gina!" Hillman shouted.

The darkness in the room had consumed Rob and he saw a flash of light as he felt his body go limp. It wasn't the welcoming tunnel of light he heard about. Just a flicker. A loud bang followed by a shriek. He crumpled to the floor and coughed as the air filled his lungs. His face and head felt wet and he couldn't see. He leaned back against a limp mass and coughed as he felt his life return to him. He tried to speak but could only croak and moan.

"Rob!" He felt some arms wrap around him, but they weren't Marvin's. He screamed from a searing pain in his neck and Gina pulled away from, gun in hand. The hot barrel had burned him. She wiped his face and her hands were red. Marvin laid next to them in a pool of his own blood. Gina slicked back Rob's hair to keep the blood from running into his eyes. He groaned and his voice returned to him.

"Am I dead?" he asked. Gina laughed through her tears.

"No, honey. You're not dead."

He looked up and Hillman put cuffs on a still dumbfounded Darlene. The boy had come down the stairs and stared at them in horror. Gina hadn't seen him yet. The grisly scene was too grotesque for a child's eyes and tears rolled down his cheeks.

"Daddy?" the boy said with a confused and frightened look. Gina whipped her head around and burst into tears. She shuffled over to him on her knees, arms spread out.

"Alex!"

The boy took a frightened step backward.

"Mommy?" He fell into her arms and wrapped his hands around her shoulders. Her hands searched all over his body as she held him. He stared at Rob and Gina pulled back from her embrace.

"Are you okay, baby?" she asked him. Alex nodded as he wiped his eyes. Rob hoisted himself up using the table and joined them. They held each other while Hillman sat Darlene down and barked into his walkie-talkie. There was no answer and he led everyone outside to his car. He placed Darlene in the back seat and locked the doors. He stomped back toward the house and put his hand on Rob's shoulder.

"Gonna go call for an ambulance and some backup." Hillman patted Rob's back and went inside. Rob just held his family close as they huddled together in the cool night air.

After a short time, Rob heard the sirens in the distance and soon the property was ablaze with flashing lights. Paramedics and county sheriffs zipped about. Rob sat on the back ledge of an ambulance and watched Gina with Alex while a responder tended to him. At no time was there less than one of Gina's hands on the boy. Rob got cleaned up and received a clean bill of health. Hillman sent Darlene away in a cruiser and collected the Marshall family.

"You guys are riding with me," he said. "I'll have you home in no time." Rob held his hand out to the detective and they shook.

"You saved my life. Thank you."

"I was only following you because I was worried about Gina. I had you all wrong, Rob. I'm sorry," Hillman said. "Plus, you shouldn't thank me. Gina's the one who put him down."

They sat in the back of Hillman's beige car, nestled close together despite their seat belts. Alex twirled Gina's hair in his fingers as they sped along the highway. Rob looked at the dashboard and saw that it was after midnight. He tapped Gina's leg and nodded to the front of the car.

"Look at the time," Rob said. Gina leaned down and kissed Alex on the head. She stroked his hair and said something Rob never thought he would hear her say again.

"Happy birthday, snuggle bug."

- 17 -

Rob sat down at his desk, ready to take on another uneventful day at work. He turned his computer on and poured himself a cup of coffee from the pot that had been sitting there since God knows when. When he sat back down, he looked at the stack of paperwork piled in his inbox. Before he got started, he stopped to look at the brand new family portrait on his desk that Gina framed for him. No matter how many times he saw it, he was elated. Alex was on his way with all the therapy and counseling. He still had nightmares and, most nights, he slept in bed with them. But that didn't bother Rob one little bit.

The office started to fill up as the overlap from the overnighters and day shift intersected. The nighthawks headed home with yawns and stretches and the bright-eyed morning people greeted each other on their way in. Rob started filling out his forms and reports for the higher-ups. It was odd that most of this stuff was still done with pen and paper in this day and age, but it was pretty relaxing compared to the usual chaos of his job. A familiar voice came from behind him.

"Don't get too cozy with that paperwork," the woman said. Rob set his pen down on the folder and sighed.

"Where are we going this time?" he said.

"Los Angeles."

He set his watch to Pacific time so he wouldn't forget to do it when they landed.

"Do we have any details?" Rob turned around and looked up at Agent Dana Brown.

"I'll fill you in on the way to the airport," she said. "Ever been to Tinseltown, Agent Marshall?"

THE END

ABOUT THE AUTHOR

Brian Colborne is a Canadian author and family man. He has worked in the fields of wireless technology and telecom as well as the financial sector.
Scattered in were stints as a bass player and songwriter in rock and heavy metal bands.
He lives with his amazing wife and two wonderful sons in London, Ontario where he grew up and hopes to stay for the rest of his life.

If you want to be the first to know when Brian releases a new book, please visit
www.bcolborne.com
and sign up to get an e-mail notification for new releases. Your e-mail will never be shared for any reason.